"I've learned the be **worth waiting for.**

"I know I'm eight years old[...] a past. I'm hoping you'll giv[...] [...]nce to get to know you better. This dinner is my way of letting you know how I feel."

Panic set in. She was the woman who'd captured Zane's interest?

But that was impossible!

Avery's fear was so great, she found herself saying it out loud.

"Why is it impossible?"

She trembled over and over again. "You don't know the real me."

Dear Reader,

Utah celebrates July 24 to honor the Pioneers who came into the Salt Lake Valley in 1847. My great-grandfather, John Brown, was among this courageous group of men and women who left their homelands across the ocean to carve out a new life. This Scotch-Irish young man had prepared to be a school teacher in the East. But unexpected circumstances brought him to the untamed American West. He was totally unprepared for the adventure awaiting him. He had to learn new skills, and learn them quickly, in order to survive. He became a cowboy.

I had John's story in mind when I wrote this latest book of the Hitting Rocks Cowboys series, *The New Cowboy*. Zane Lawson, born in San Francisco, had been a Navy SEAL. He'd thought it would be his lifetime career, but he, too, encountered unexpected circumstances that brought him to the wilds of Montana. It may be the twenty-first century, but he is forced to embrace a future totally foreign to him and adapt as fast as he can. In the process he morphs into *The New Cowboy*, who has a special skill—bringing healing to Avery Bannock, the beautiful woman he loves.

Enjoy!

Rebecca Winters

THE NEW COWBOY

———

REBECCA WINTERS

HARLEQUIN® AMERICAN ROMANCE®

Recycling programs
for this product may
not exist in your area.

ISBN-13: 978-0-373-75551-6

The New Cowboy

Copyright © 2015 by Rebecca Winters

Printed in U.S.A.

www.Harlequin.com

Rebecca Winters, whose family of four children has now swelled to include five beautiful grandchildren, lives in Salt Lake City, Utah, in the land of the Rocky Mountains. With canyons and high alpine meadows full of wildflowers, she never runs out of places to explore. They, plus her favorite vacation spots in Europe, often end up as backgrounds for her romance novels, because writing is her passion, along with her family and church.

Rebecca loves to hear from readers.
If you wish to email her, please visit her website:
www.cleanromances.com.

Books by Rebecca Winters

HARLEQUIN AMERICAN ROMANCE

Hitting Rocks Cowboys Series

In a Cowboy's Arms
A Cowboy's Heart

Daddy Dude Ranch Series

The Wyoming Cowboy
Home to Wyoming
Her Wyoming Hero

Undercover Heroes Series

The SEAL's Promise
The Marshal's Prize
The Texas Ranger's Reward

This and other titles by Rebecca Winters are also available in ebook format from www.Harlequin.com.

To my great-grandfather, Pioneer John Brown, Captain of the Thirteenth Ten, who crossed the plains ten times, bringing more and more Pioneers out West. He was a son, husband, father and patriarch, who befriended members of the Ute Indian tribe, served in the Utah Legislature and helped settle parts of Southern Utah. His image is on the This Is The Place Monument in Salt Lake, riding his horse and carrying his Kentucky rifle. What a cowboy!

Chapter One

"Unca Zen!"

Zane laughed. "Hey, sport. I can see you on my computer. Can you see me?"

"Yes."

"Did you get those little cars I sent you?"

"I like this one." The three-year-old held it up for Zane to see. As far as he was concerned, Skype was the best cyberinvention ever.

"Say thank-you to your uncle," he heard Sadie say in the background.

"Thank you. When are you coming?"

"Pretty soon. I still have work to do."

"But I want you to come home!"

Zane could tell his brother's son was getting ready to cry.

He got a huge lump in his throat. "There's nothing I want more, too. Guess what?"

"What?"

"I'll be there for my vacation on the Fourth of July." Three weeks away. He was living for it. "We're going to have a big party with fireworks at my house!"

"Goody!" Ryan turned to Sadie. "What's fireworks?"

"She'll show you, sport. Has Jarod taken you riding?"

The boy nodded his blond head. "The horse scared me. He's huge."

Laughter poured out of Zane. "They are kind of big."

"I'm getting a pony."

"When?"

"Pretty soon," Sadie volunteered.

"You'll be a very lucky boy."

Zane heard her whispering to Ryan. "She says I have to go to bed. I don't want to!" He started crying.

"But you need your sleep."

"No— I want you—"

"Say good-night, Ryan."

"No-o—"

Zane heard talking in the background. Ryan was becoming more unmanageable. Someone else had come into the room. He could hear Sadie saying they had to go.

"Don't go, Unca Zen—" Ryan wailed, sounding like his heart would break.

Sadie poked her head into view. "Sorry. This little guy is tired."

"I can tell. Who's there with you?"

"Avery just dropped by."

His adrenaline kicked in. "Put her on."

"Just a minute." He heard more talking. "Come on over here, Avery. Zane wants to say hello. Tell him what's going on at the Bannock ranch while I put Ryan down."

The boy was in complete meltdown mode as they left the room. His nephew's cries grew fainter and Zane's heart started pounding harder as he waited to see the woman who kept him awake nights.

His breath caught when she sat down in front of the camera. "Hi, Zane. I guess you can't tell your nephew adores you."

"The feeling's mutual. How are you?"

"Good. Busy. I'm surprised you've come out from undercover long enough to manage this Skype session."

"I'll always make time for my family."

"Now that you've been working there for a while, do you like the Glasgow area?"

"It's all right, but I'd rather be back on my ranch. Matt has the whole burden on his shoulders when I'm away like this."

"He carried most of it all the years he worked for Daniel Corkin. I don't hear any complaints."

"Matt isn't the type to complain. I'm lucky he was willing to be my foreman after Daniel died. But let's not talk about that. I want to know what's happening in your world."

"Since Jarod's not home yet, and it'll be a while before Ryan goes to sleep, I'll tell you a secret. Jarod is driving us all crazy waiting for his offspring to arrive. He's due in five weeks. I swear Jarod's going to wear a hole in the floor of their new house."

"He's still worried about Sadie?"

"More than ever. I've never seen him this bad. I

know she's had a lot of morning sickness, but the doctor says she's fine. Jarod doesn't believe him."

"I guess that's not so hard to understand. Sadie's mom died soon after childbirth."

"But Sadie's not her mom. That heart operation was successful and she's fine now. But you can't tell Jarod that. He bites your head off. We have to walk on eggshells around him. He used to work all hours of the day on the ranch. Now he comes home every few hours, and the rest of the time he's on the phone with her."

"The man's in love." Zane could relate in the most profound of ways.

"Between you and me, he's driving her crazy."

"But never too crazy. Trust me on that. When she was in San Francisco, he was never off her mind for a single second. Those two should have been together years ago."

You and I should be together now.

"I know. I try not to think about that. But this countdown to the baby is getting hard on everyone. The other day Grandpa got so fed up he told him to take a ride in the mountains and commune with nature. It's gotten so serious even Uncle Charlo has no wisdom to impart. When I was out on the reservation the other day and talked to him about Jarod, he actually shook his head, indicating he had nothing. I've never seen him do that before."

"Well, it won't be long before the baby comes."

"That's easy for you to say. You're not here to watch Jarod implode on a daily basis."

Zane burst into laughter, causing her to chuckle.

"I'll give him a call and try to reassure him that Sadie's tough."

"I've seen that strength. She's already become a mother to her own half brother. Sadie has a remarkable capacity to love. Jarod relies on that love. It's really touching to watch the two of them."

The wistfulness in her tone wasn't lost on Zane, who couldn't take the separation from Avery much longer.

"I'm afraid I need to get off now. Grandpa is waiting for me."

No-o—

Zane felt exactly like Ryan. "I guess I'll be seeing all of you on the Fourth of July for the big family get-together."

"It'll be fun. I've enjoyed talking to you, Zane. Hold on while I tiptoe to Ryan's room. Sadie will want to say good-night." There was a slight pause. "Take care," she said with a throb in her voice he felt go through his system. It was always there…that little nuance of emotion that told him she missed him, but she'd never admit it.

"The same back to you, Avery."

ANOTHER MONDAY MORNING, but it had started out with a surprise phone call that left Avery Bannock frightened and tense. She'd had to leave the Crow Indian dig site where she was working outside Absarokee, Montana, and drive all the way to Bozeman, Montana.

Once inside the police department on Sixteenth Street, she approached the sergeant at the front desk. "A Detective Rymer phoned me two hours ago and asked me to come in because he needed to tell me certain information in person. He said it was urgent." After hearing that message, the warm June morning she'd awakened to had been lost on her.

The officer nodded. "Go down the left hall to the first door on the right."

"Thank you."

She hadn't been inside this building for eight years, but the emergency that had brought her here would haunt her for her entire life. "Detective Rymer?"

He stood up when she entered the small office. "Ms. Bannock?"

"Yes."

"I'm glad you came so fast." He shook her hand and asked her to be seated. "Detective Palmer, who has worked tirelessly on your case, is having back surgery at the moment and asked me to take over for him."

"Was he injured in the line of duty?"

"No. He has a recurring ailment that needed to be fixed."

"I'm glad that's the reason, but I'm sorry for him. He's been a great support to me."

"To you and a lot of people. We're all waiting for him to come back."

"You said this was urgent?"

"Very. I'll get right to the point. The man who assaulted you on September 10, eight years ago, outside the women's dormitory on campus at Montana State University, was captured in Helena, Montana, last week."

What? She reeled. "Is that the truth?"

"Forensics matched his DNA with the DNA taken from you and two other victims."

Two others? She shuddered. "I can't believe it! After eight years…"

"I'm sure it has seemed like a lifetime. He's a thirty-nine-year-old Caucasian male from Butte, Montana. In the past eight years he's been responsible for two other assaults that the police know of and probably many more.

"Unfortunately those victims who didn't go to a hospital and notify the police will never know that he's been arrested. After his trial he'll spend the rest of his life in prison. If there's any good news in all this, it's that you no longer need to fear that he will be back to assault you again."

She put a hand to her mouth and jumped up from the chair. *"Thank God."*

"All the particulars are here in the report if you want to look at it."

"No—" she said. "Not right now. I couldn't." Though she'd promised that she would be willing to testify against the person if he was ever brought to trial, the thought of having to divulge all the details again in front of a room full of people made her ill.

He eyed her with compassion. "I understand. Detective Palmer will want to talk to you when he's recovered. He'll be the one to keep you informed when the suspect is brought to trial for his crimes. You can discuss all that with him when he's back on his feet."

"Thank you."

Avery rushed out of the office and down the corridor to the front lobby, but everything was a blur. When she reached her truck in the parking lot and climbed inside, she broke down in a convulsion of tears.

A half hour passed before she lifted her head, once again aware of her surroundings. Pulling herself together as best she could, she reached for her cell phone and called Dr. Moser, her psychologist. When she got the other woman on the line and told her the incredible news, the doctor who practiced on the other side of town asked her to come to her office straightaway.

Once inside, Dr. Moser enveloped her in a fierce hug, causing Avery to shed more tears when she hadn't thought it possible. "I don't have to be frightened that he's stalking me any longer."

"That's true and takes away a whole world of stress."

Avery sat down. "But not all of it," she admitted.

"No. With two other victims, there will be a trial and then you'll have to decide if you want to go through it and face him. For now it's enough to know he's been caught. I can't tell you how proud I am of you. Only a small percentage of victims come forward. How wonderful that you listened to your half brother's aunt and did the right thing by calling the police right away and getting to a hospital."

One day Avery would thank Jarod's Aunt Pauline for her wisdom. By listening to her, she now had closure, even if it had taken eight years for her assailant to be caught.

"You have a special kind of courage that's going to get you through this life. Mark my words. One day you're going to know real happiness again. With this news you can live your life without always having to look over your shoulder in fear. I'll call the pharmacy in White Lodge and refill your prescription. Is there anything else I can do?"

"You've been here for me. I'll always be thankful for that."

Avery had been fighting to get her life back since the night the assault had happened, but this news was like receiving a "get out of jail free" card, even if it couldn't take away the horrendous memory of it.

She thanked the doctor and left for the dig site. Work helped her keep her sanity, especially on a day like this when she didn't know what to do with all the new emotions flooding her system. It was so automatic to worry that her assailant might try to attack her again that she'd probably continue to worry out of habit for a long time. Hopefully the news that he'd been caught would finally sink in.

All these years of fearing he would target her again had left their mark. Now that it was over, she could breathe a little deeper. But since there were other assailants out there, the fear would never completely go away.

Today had to be a new beginning—the start of a happy future—but she still couldn't comprehend it. Happiness was found in all kinds of ways, but she feared that the kind of joy she longed for with the man she'd loved for the past year would always elude her. After talking to him over Skype at Sadie and Jarod's ranch house the other night, her thoughts had been filled with him.

He was coming home for the Fourth of July, but it was just a vacation. Then he'd go back to northern Montana where he'd be unavailable for who knew how many months. But none of it mattered because even if he was attracted to her, he wouldn't be able to handle what had happened to her if he ever found out.

THURSDAY MORNING, ZANE LAWSON left the Bureau of Land Management's office of Law Enforcement and Security in Glasgow, Montana, where he'd been an undercover special agent, and headed for the parking lot. Once he'd climbed into his unmarked blue four-door Dodge Power Wagon without government plates, he started the engine and headed for Billings.

En route he phoned the Corkin ranch he'd bought a year ago near the Montana-Wyoming border. He needed to talk to his foreman, Matt Henson.

Matt and his wife, Millie, lived in the house next door to the Corkin ranch house. She did the housekeeping for Zane. They were both salt of the earth people. Since a little over a year ago when he'd first come to Montana from San Francisco with his stepniece, Sadie, and his nephew, Ryan, Zane had grown to look upon Matt and Millie as family.

"Hey, Matt—"

"Zane? What's going on? I thought you were out on a case and couldn't be reached for a while."

"That sting produced results at long last and now I'm coming home."

"For how long?"

"Permanently."

Zane could hear Matt's mind turning things over. "What kind of permanently do you mean? Is that good or bad?"

"Oh, it's good. After cleaning up a drug ring that had been plaguing the area for a long time, the transfer I asked for came through to work in the Pryor Mountains area. The lead state ranger in Billings just phoned to let me know I've been assigned to the Billings office. They've added a bonus I never expected."

"What's that?"

"I'll be running a satellite station for the BLM Law Enforcement Division right here at the ranch."

After being in the grasslands around Glasgow at the northern end of the state, the thought of going home to the mountains thrilled him. He'd missed three-year-old Ryan and the ranch so badly he could taste it. Their latest Skype session that had included Avery had been hard on him.

"You'll be working from the *ranch*?" Matt wasn't one for drama, but after hearing about the transfer, he let go with a long ear piercing whistle. "That's the best news I ever heard."

Zane smiled. "No. I'm pretty sure the best news came the day your rodeo champion daughter married Connor Bannock. But now I'll be on hand to do the ranching with you more often."

"You'll be just in time to help me calve out the heifers from the herd."

"Yeah? I'm looking forward to it more than you know. How's Millie?"

"She's going to be higher than a kite when she hears this."

"I'm pretty happy, too." The opportunity to buy the Corkin ranch where Sadie had been raised had come at the same time he'd left the SEALs to work for the Bureau of Land Management—both changes had turned his life around. With two viable careers, one of them ranching in the area of Montana he loved, he could plan for his future and put down roots. "How are the lovebirds?"

"Which pair of newlyweds are we talking about?"

Zane chuckled. "Both!"

"I do believe Lizzie and Sadie have found their soul mates."

"That's a fact."

Zane hadn't been so lucky. Besides being in a marriage that had grown troubled, his wife, Nedra, had been unfaithful to him. He'd retired from a ten-year stint in the Navy SEALs and divorced her. After that his older brother, Tim, his only living blood relative, was killed in a car crash. That left Tim's pregnant wife, Eileen, Sadie's mother. But after giving birth, Eileen soon died unexpectedly of heart failure.

Too many deaths…

Together he and Sadie took care of little Ryan. Just eighteen months ago, he'd been jobless, homeless and womanless. He hadn't known what direction to take with his life. Then fate had stepped in to change everything.

"You should see Sadie," Matt went on. "She has blossomed with her pregnancy. Once Jarod found out they were having a boy, you can imagine the grin on his face."

Sadie's husband wasn't the type to grin. It told you everything. Jarod and Sadie were raising Ryan as their own and now a new son was on the way.

With a smile he asked, "How's the Queen of the Rodeo?" That was what Avery's brother, Connor, called his wife, Liz. The famous five-time World Steer Wrestling Champion was crazy about his new wife.

"She and Connor have started advertising their feral stud farm. Talk about two people meant for each other. They built their new house near Jarod's and will be moving into it this Saturday. Ralph Bannock is so happy these days, he's put on some weight and gets out every day. Having both of his grandsons home and married has given him a new lease on life."

"That's a miracle."

"It sure is. When you and Sadie flew here with Ryan for her father's funeral a year ago May, Ralph couldn't get out of bed. So much has changed since you came to Montana for Corkin's funeral—it's unbelievable."

Everything had changed, including Zane. He had one more question and had been saving it for last, but his pulse was pounding. "How's Avery these days?" The Avery she'd always kept hidden from him. Those Bannock brothers had a beautiful sister who'd knocked him sideways the first time he'd met her.

"She's fine, but we don't see much of her."

That sounded like Avery. She was an elusive creature with brown hair and unforgettable crystalline gray eyes. The nature of his work had made it impossible for him to be around her on a regular basis and really get to know her.

When he did get some time with her, she seemed nervous around him. He didn't understand her reaction because he knew deep down she was attracted. There were times he felt her eyes on him when she thought he wasn't looking. Now that he was coming home, he planned to get to the bottom of it and was determined things were going to change.

He was so deep in thought about her, he didn't realize Matt was still talking to him. "Zane? Are you still there? Can you hear me?"

"Yes. Sorry. I got distracted for a minute. I'll be driving in sometime tonight, probably around seven-thirty." The distance to White Lodge, the nearest town to the ranch, was a good three hundred and forty miles. "I have to make a stop in Billings first."

"Be sure to drive safely because we'll all be waiting for you."

"Thanks, Matt."

He clicked off and increased his speed. While he'd been in Glasgow, he'd constantly wondered if Avery might have fallen for someone he didn't know about. But Sadie, who was close to her sister-in-law, kept in touch with him by email and she hadn't said anything to that effect.

During his Skype sessions with Sadie, which let him talk to his nephew and see how he was growing, he always hoped Avery was there. Occasionally she happened to show up. On Monday, he'd devoured her with his eyes as they talked. Every time they spoke, it made him hungrier for her.

She'd been the only woman to stir Zane's senses since his divorce. But as he'd found out on the day of Daniel Corkin's funeral, her guard went up around Zane. He figured she'd seen him as an outsider at first and that was why she didn't let him in. Yet when she was around her brothers, she was a completely different person, warm and loving.

He found it unbelievable that such a desirable woman wasn't involved with someone special. In talking with Sadie he'd learned that Avery had dated a little in high school. Evidently she preferred to be off riding in the mountains and spending time on the Crow Indian Reservation. After high school she went to Montana State University in Bozeman for her undergraduate degree. Later she received a graduate fellowship from the anthropology department at Berkeley in California.

Zane could only speculate about her social life during that six-year period before she returned home to work these past two years. His thoughts flew back to the time he'd lived at the Bannock ranch house for two weeks. Sadie and Jarod had spent their honeymoon on the Corkin ranch so they could be near her half brother, Ryan, while the Hensons helped tend him.

Zane had moved out temporarily to accommodate them and took over Jarod's bedroom on the second floor down the hall from Avery's bedroom. During those two weeks, Zane shared his meals with Avery and her grandfather in the morning and evening.

They'd mostly discussed ranch life and her work

with the Crow people who lived on the reservation. Not only was she intelligent, she had a great love for the Crow culture, no doubt due to Jarod's deceased Crow mother.

Connor and Avery shared a different mother. After Jarod's mother died, his father met another woman and married her. Two children came from that marriage, Connor and Avery. From the beginning it was clear Avery worshipped her older brothers and the three of them were tight in every way.

Avery had depths he hadn't found in other women. She did ranching chores with her brothers and could ride a horse like Sadie and Liz. In fact she could do a lot of things a vet could do. Her remarkable talents and the desire for academic learning that had earned her a master's degree made her exceptional in his eyes.

During those two weeks they'd played cards with Ralph and were starting to get to know each other better when his application to join the BLM was approved and he was sent to Georgia for law enforcement training. After being in the SEALs, it was like déjà vu.

But in one day Zane had to pack his bags and go. When his training was over, he was temporarily assigned to the field office in Glasgow, cutting off his chance to spend more time with her. Though his instincts told him she wanted to be with him, something was holding her back from expressing her interest openly. She was a mystery that wanted solving.

He picked up lunch at a drive-through before entering the field office in Billings. While he ate, he listened to the noon news.

…And there's still no news about the explosives heist. Last week we reported that five hundred pounds of explosives had been stolen from a locked federal storage facility near Billings, Montana. Federal officials do not believe it's terrorism-related, but it has raised security issues.

Montana's only congressman was quoted as saying, "I'm deeply concerned about the theft and will be closely monitoring the investigation."

Zane frowned and turned up the volume to listen while he finished off his hamburger.

The thieves took off with various emulsion-type explosives, cast boosters and detonating cord. Federal officials aren't able to point to why the explosives were taken and have downplayed what could happen if they fall into the wrong hands.

Some in the area—who don't want to be named publicly—believe the facility might have been looted by local miners or by private forestry-related companies that want to bypass buying the explosives legally. The local sheriff says they don't have any idea who did it, but the types of items taken are used in mines and to clear rock slides and construction trails.

The latest news flash on the heist was the first thing the lead ranger Sanders talked about after they shook hands. "Welcome to Billings and your first case."

Zane chuckled.

"The spokesman for the Bureau of Alcohol, Tobacco, Firearms and Explosives said they're offering a five-thousand-dollar reward for information and the culprit will be given ten years of prison time. There've been no arrests yet."

"I'll do my best."

"We're pleased to have you assigned to our team, Lawson. That drug trafficking ring you put away has rid the state of a real menace. Congratulations on your special commendation from the top brass. With your background in the SEALs, no one's surprised you've surpassed expectations."

"Thank you."

"From now on you'll be conducting criminal and civil investigations into various types of crimes spreading through eight counties associated with our field office. Besides pursuing investigations for cultivation of marijuana, fraud, arson and assaults on BLM employees, you'll be looking into thefts of archaeological and paleontological resources. More and more of that is going on.

"Just today we had another call from the local police concerning more vandalism and thefts at one of the dig sites. Some of these crimes are broad in scope, involving interstate transport of stolen artifacts. Many of your investigations will require you to work outside your assigned area. Don't be surprised if you're asked to join a task force for interagency operations and security."

"Understood."

"With this latest theft, I trust you're ready for more trouble."

"To be honest, I'm anxious to get started on some new cases."

Sanders broke out in a smile. "The SEALs loss is our gain." He got to his feet. "I know you're on your way home so I won't detain you. Before the day is out, I'll email some of the recent cases involving geovandalism and felony mischief to you. Call me anytime."

"I will. Thank you."

He hurried out to his truck, anxious to get home. Six months ago he'd flown down to the National Finals Rodeo in Las Vegas with Sadie and her husband to watch Liz and Connor compete. Avery had come with her family.

They'd all partied after the competition and she'd seemed to enjoy his company while everyone was around. They'd danced for several hours, long enough for a fire to have been lit. If they happened to be alone she kept him at arm's length, yet the chemistry between them was stronger than ever. Unfortunately he'd had to get right back to Glasgow.

Under the circumstances, any relationship had to be put off while he was still working in the northern part of the state. Though he'd been home a few times since then and had gotten together with her and both families, he needed more time alone with her.

A half smile broke the corner of his mouth. Now that his transfer had come through, he was going to get all the time he wanted. After all, they were next-door neighbors from here on out.

Chapter Two

Avery loved the month of June. After coming out of freezing winter, night didn't come until late and the mountains sprang to colorful life with wildflowers. But lovely as it was to have the warm sun following her home to the ranch on this Thursday evening, the balmier weather brought out vandals and thieves who desecrated the archaeological sites.

The one she'd been working on outside Absarokee had been hit again, infuriating her. She and the team spent hours out there, so careful not to destroy one millimeter of soil in order not to corrupt the ground holding precious information. Then during the night their work was set back by thugs and lowlifes.

During the thirty-minute drive home, the helplessness she felt over the situation had caught up with her and she needed to calm down. Mike Durant would be coming to the ranch for her soon. He'd driven by the site to make arrangements for tonight. They were going to dinner in White Lodge. For several months he'd been dropping by the site to talk to her about her work and had asked her out repeatedly.

She'd finally accepted and they'd had one dinner date. But this second date would have to be their final one. He'd asked her out again in front of the other team members and she hadn't wanted to embarrass him by turning him down. Though she didn't want to hurt his pride, she couldn't go out with him again. It was a mistake she'd regretted from the moment he'd tried to turn friendship into something else.

Earlier in the month when Liz Bannock had learned that Avery had gone out on a first date with him, her new sister-in-law had eyed her with the kind of excitement that made her uncomfortable. "What's he like?" Funny about happily married people. They wanted everyone else to find their soul mate and settle down.

"Nice, but I can see what's in your eyes, Liz, and it's not going to happen."

Her expression deflated. "What's wrong?"

"I like him, but—"

"But what?" Liz prodded.

"I'm not interested." On the advice of her psychologist, Avery had accepted a date with Mike in order to get back in the dating loop, but it hadn't worked and now she was paying for it.

"I thought you found him attractive."

"I did in a way. He works for the Bureau of Indian Affairs and he's a good source of information because of his work among other tribes." That much was true. "He's well-informed about the Crow culture, kind of like Jarod."

"Wait a minute—you mean you were drawn to him

because he reminds you of Sits in the Center?" That was Jarod's Crow name.

Avery and her brothers shared the same father, but his first wife, Raven, was from the Crow Nation. After Jarod was born, she died. Later he married another woman named Maddie, who was Connor and Avery's mother.

"Only in a certain sense, but after one date I discovered Mike is nothing like Jarod. He's nice, but that's all." Mike was too aggressive.

Growing up, Avery had worshipped her big brother and everyone knew it. On more than one occasion she'd told her sisters-in-law and her cousin Cassie that she'd never get married unless she found a man she loved more than she loved Jarod. It was an easy excuse that still worked these days on those who were concerned about Avery's almost nonexistent love life.

No one knew that a year ago May, love had hit her with the force of a supernova when Zane Lawson happened on the scene. But like the heavens, he was beyond her reach and would remain her secret.

Unfortunately Liz wouldn't let it go. She shook her head. "I don't believe you. What's the real reason you don't want to see Mike again?"

"To be honest, there's something about his personality that turns me off."

"That's too bad. It makes me sad because I'm worried about you."

She had to tamp down a burst of temper. "Not everyone is lucky enough to find the kind of happiness you've found with Connor." To have a normal life was something that had escaped Avery, but the news from Detective Rymer had taken away a gargantuan shadow. With it gone, she had to face a new reality. Her feelings for Zane ran so deep, the last thing she wanted was to give another guy hope that she was interested in him. Especially not Mike.

"We're not talking about me." Liz refused to be put off. "I'm serious, Avery. There's been something wrong with you since you first went away to college in Bozeman. When are you going to break down and tell me what it is?"

Never.

Avery had her therapist in Bozeman, whom she'd been seeing for the past eight years, and she didn't need anyone else. No one but Dr. Moser and the police knew Avery's secret and that was the way it would stay even though she loved Liz with all her heart. "Please don't worry about me."

"I can't help it. That's what family is for."

Liz was a sweetheart, but no one could help with Avery's particular problem rooted deep in the past. If time could dim the pain, then she'd pray for that much relief.

Now Avery pulled the truck around the side of the ranch house and hurried through the terrace to the dining room where she found her grandfather Ralph. He was talking on the phone while he ate his dinner.

When he saw her, he ended the call. "There's my Avery. Come here, darlin'."

She leaned over to give him a hug. "Hi, Grandpa. How have you been today?"

"Never better."

"You've been doing so much better lately." Her eyes teared up. She adored the man who'd taken over as both parent and grandparent after her parents had died. "I'm so thankful."

He squeezed her hand. "Me, too. Guess what? I've just received exciting news from Matt."

Now that there'd been another marriage in the family, her grandfather and Matt Henson had become best friends, the way it should always have been. Watching the national rodeo finals together on the television had bonded the families in new ways.

Avery needed to shower, but she sat down for a minute to hear him out. "Tell me what's going on."

His eyes lit up. "The owner of the Corkin ranch is coming home tonight for good."

"You must be mistaken, Grandpa. He'll be here on the Fourth of July for his vacation. Not before."

He shook his head. "You didn't listen to me. I said he's coming home for good tonight."

The news caused the blood to pound in her ears like thunder over the Pryors. *Zane Lawson was coming back?* "What do you mean for good?" Her voice faltered.

"He's been transferred from Glasgow to the Billings field office. There's more. They've authorized him to set up a satellite BLM criminal law enforcement office at the ranch so he can cover the Pryor Mountains region from home. He's back to stay and I'm ecstatic!"

Avery shot to her feet. "You're joking." He'd be working next door from now on?

"I wouldn't joke about a thing like that. Matt and Millie couldn't be more delighted." Her grandfather went on talking. He had no idea what was going on inside Avery. "This will thrill Sadie. Ryan asks about his uncle Zane every day."

Avery knew about that. Often when she went to Sadie's, her sister-in-law was on Skype with Zane so he and his nephew could see and talk to each other. Last week was a revelation. Ryan had thrown a tantrum because he hadn't wanted to stop talking to Zane.

Neither had Avery, who loved those rare, precious moments. She'd never been able to get enough of Zane. Sadie would include Avery so that she and Zane could communicate. Her pulse raced during those sessions.

Now he was coming home for good. Avery was so staggered by the revelation, she was trembling. That little boy adored him. So did Sadie. So did everyone who knew Zane.

So did Avery.

"That's wonderful news, but right now I've got to get ready."

"What for?"

"Mike Durant is coming by to take me to dinner."

"Is he an archaeologist?"

"No. He works for the Bureau of Indian Affairs."

Her grandfather scrutinized her. "How come I never heard of him? Do you like him?"

"He's all right."

"When did you meet him?"

"After Christmas. He was transferred from the office on the Pawnee Reservation in Nebraska, but we can talk about it later." Her heart was racing with unhealthy speed. "Does Jarod know about Zane?"

"I'm going to call them right now. Matt's already told Liz and Connor. Millie's planned a party for everyone later tonight. Too bad you can't be with us. Zane's the finest man I know."

That was high praise coming from her grandfather. "Do you need me to drive you over before I leave?"

"Oh, no. One of the boys will take me. You go on and have a good time."

Smothering a groan, Avery kissed his cheek. Her grandfather's news about Zane had shaken her so badly she ran out of the room and up the stairs to her bedroom to get ahold of herself. After removing her snap-up Western shirt, she took off the holster shirt that concealed her pistol. It was a lightweight Beretta Nano pocketed under the left arm. She set it on the dresser and got in the shower.

Avery couldn't believe Zane was back. Ralph's praise of him rang in her ears. Little did her grandfather know she thought Zane was the finest man *she'd* ever known. Heroic. Honorable. Exciting. Fascinating. A man to match the mountains she loved. *And desirable beyond belief.*

But soul-destroying fear nipped at the heels of her excitement that he was coming home, ruining the news for her. During her years of therapy, Dr. Moser had helped Avery get to the point where she could trust again and accept going out on dates. After the assault, that was progress. But the psychologist predicted that one day a man would come along who would make

Avery feel the deep emotions of desire and intense wanting she'd thought had died.

As Dr. Moser pointed out, in order to have a full, loving physical and emotional relationship with this person, Avery would have to end the silence and tell him the truth about the assault on her.

Avery hadn't been able to imagine the day coming when she'd meet such a man. And when and if she did, how would she overcome the shame, humiliation, depression, anger, fear? The guilt. It had been eight years and yet she was still suffering to some degree from all those emotions, especially shame.

After her attack, she'd called the police from the hospital. Jarod's aunt Pauline, a nurse on the reservation, had always worried about Avery riding in the mountains and on the reservation alone. She'd continually warned her that if, heaven forbid she was ever assaulted, she should go to the hospital immediately for a thorough examination in order for the police to catch the culprit.

When Avery thought about it, Pauline had given her amazing counsel years ago. But maybe it wasn't so amazing after all. If she, too, had the gift of vision like her husband, Charlo, it was possible she'd sensed something about Avery's future and had warned her. According to Pauline, there were too many assaults on the reservation. Being on duty at the hospital, she saw a lot of things and had shared that information with her.

On the night of Avery's assault, Pauline's advice had rung in her ears. She went to the hospital and the collected evidence and DNA had been entered in her file to help the police. Since that time she'd prayed every day that her assailant would be caught so he couldn't hurt anyone else, but in all the years since, there'd been no news until Monday.

The doctor at the hospital had helped her find the right psychologist. Within a few days she'd started self-defense classes and had bought a handgun she learned to shoot. Her concealed weapons permit allowed her a certain amount of protection. She was doing all she could to prevent herself from being victimized again. But if she told Zane the truth about her traumatic experience, it would turn him off.

He was too good a man to be interested in a woman like Avery. On occasion in his line of work as an agent, he had to arrest criminals inflicting that kind of horror on their victims. She could only imagine the kind of taste it left in his mouth. Avery couldn't bear the thought of him having to put her in that category.

When Zane had walked into the room at the funeral for Sadie's father, Avery hadn't been able to take her eyes off him. Everything about him excited her to the very core of her being and she knew she'd met the man her therapist had been talking about.

His tall, hard-muscled physique had created a stir among all the women gathered there. At first everyone, including Avery, thought the brooding, retired Navy SEAL was Sadie's lover from California. Before Jarod knew differently, it had almost destroyed him to see Sadie with Zane.

Beneath dark brown hair and eyebrows, his startling blue gaze had swept the living room at the Corkin ranch without really seeing anyone. He'd seemed totally removed from the event and had gathered Sadie's little half brother in his strong arms to entertain him away from the others.

It was when he'd smiled at his nephew, Ryan, that his hard-boned features gave way to faint dimples, melting Avery on the spot. In that moment he'd looked up at her and the world reeled away. The male admiration in his eyes lit up every cell in her body and she was never the same after that.

As Liz had remarked later that day, there wasn't a female in Montana who could be immune to such a gorgeous man. If Liz hadn't been madly in love with Connor since high school...

After meeting Zane, Sadie's divorced stepuncle, Avery learned he'd decided to stay in Montana rather than return to San Francisco. She'd be seeing him coming and going from the Corkin ranch.

Shocked by her intense attraction to him, Avery fought it in the only way she knew how and plunged into her work with more zeal than ever. For her to have to divulge those traumatic ten minutes to anyone besides the therapist made her sick inside. But when that someone was a fabulous man like Zane Lawson, she shrank from considering it.

During Sadie's honeymoon, Zane had lived at the Bannock ranch house for two weeks. Avery did her best to be friendly, but the thought of encouraging him was overshadowed by the trauma of her past. Mentally, Avery knew she didn't have anything to feel guilty about, but emotionally she was crippled. She felt soiled by it.

When Zane went to work for BLM law enforcement in Glasgow, part of her had been relieved, yet secretly the other part of her was devastated that he was so far away. Five months later she'd spent one evening with him and the family in Las Vegas. She'd felt his desire when they'd gone dancing with the others, but even though her fire for him burned hotter than ever, she'd made certain they weren't alone together.

She flew home from the trip to Nevada resolved to throw herself into one of her Crow projects, hoping to put Zane from her mind. A while back she'd finally accepted a date with Mike Durant.

Unfortunately she realized she shouldn't have accepted because it had been for the wrong reasons. Zane filled her mind and heart. She couldn't possibly go on seeing Mike when there was no attraction on her end. The only thing to do was refuse to go out with him again after tonight. But how to do it without hurting his feelings was a tall order. He'd be there any minute.

Zane would be arriving at his ranch any minute, and he wouldn't be leaving again.

She could hardly breathe.

TWILIGHT HAD CREPT over the landscape as Zane drove down the road toward the Corkin ranch. This was the kind of evening that called to him. He felt alive and excited. In thirteen months' time this place had become home to him even though he'd been away a good part of it. The few short visits had only made him long to stay put.

Out of the corner of his eye he saw a ruby-red Silverado parked in front of the Bannock ranch house. It had the Department of the Interior logo for the BIA. Must be someone from the reservation looking for Jarod and asking for directions to his new house.

Suddenly Zane saw Avery come out the front door and down the porch steps with a dark-haired man Zane didn't recognize. Something about the way he cupped her elbow told him he wasn't there on official business.

Zane's stomach knotted as he slowed down to get a better look. She'd dressed in jeans and a leaf-green Western shirt. In cowboy boots she was five foot seven. He was stunned by the feminine picture she made with her rich sable-colored hair pulled back at the nape.

In a different frame of mind than he was a moment ago, he drove on, but he kept his eyes trained on the rearview mirror. Before he turned into the ranch, he watched the truck disappear in the other direction.

How long had *that* been going on?

Forced to swallow his disappointment, he gunned the accelerator and pulled in the driveway too fast. It forced him to stand on his brakes when he reached the ranch house. With everyone's trucks parked to the side along with his Volvo, it looked like a gathering of the clan. They'd obviously been waiting for him because everyone came pouring out the front door. A Sadie who looked about ready to deliver led Ryan by the hand.

"Welcome home!" she cried. "This little guy has been waiting for you."

"Come here, sport." He reached for his nephew who was growing to look more and more like Zane's older brother, Tim. Already his hair was going darker. Zane hugged him hard and kissed him. "You have no idea how much I've missed you."

"Zen," he mispronounced his name, causing everyone to laugh.

The family took turns hugging him before Connor and Jarod brought in his bags from the truck. Because he'd lived in a furnished rental unit in Glasgow, he didn't have much else to bring home besides clothes and a laptop. It reminded him of being in the SEALs when he could be transferred in the twinkling of an eye and had no baggage but his gear.

He kissed Liz before turning to Sadie with a grin. "Judging from the look of you, it won't be long before Little Sits in the Center makes his entrance." Everyone laughed and went in the house.

Ralph was already drinking punch in the easy chair and lifted his cup to him. "It's wonderful to know you're home for good, Zane."

They shook hands. "It feels good. You look well and younger."

Ralph beamed while Zane surveyed the room, inhaling the warmth and love. Only one person was missing to make his homecoming complete.

Millie had laid out a spread fit for a king. Still carrying his nephew, he snagged her around the waist and gave her a special hug. "You have no idea how much I've missed your cooking and our card games."

She chuckled. "You're a sight for sore eyes, Zane."

Matt called everyone together. "This is a time of real celebration. We couldn't be happier with your news. While we eat, we want to hear details about your latest capture. It was all over the media and the newspapers. Talk about proud."

Zane hadn't experienced this sense of family for years. He'd lost his parents ages ago. After that his marriage had fallen apart and he'd lost Tim, then Eileen. If he hadn't had Sadie and Ryan, he didn't know where he'd be today. If it hadn't been for Sadie, he would never have met Avery Bannock.

The little guy hugged his shoulder for the next hour while they all talked and ate. But when he finally fell asleep, Jarod walked over and reached for him. "We'd better get him home to bed while he's crashed. Come on over in the morning and have breakfast with us."

Seeing Jarod with Ryan, you'd never know he wasn't the boy's father from birth. Naturally Ryan had Sadie's looks. Tim's son was in loving hands. "Sounds good."

The party broke up. Zane followed Jarod out to his truck and helped Sadie inside. Jarod put Ryan in the car seat. Once they were settled, Zane approached Jarod's side of the truck. In a quiet voice he said, "I saw a BIA agent in front of your house with Avery while I was driving in. I didn't realize she was seeing someone. They should have come over to the party." Might as well find out the strength of Zane's competition.

Jarod's inscrutable expression made it impossible to read him at times. All he said was, "Avery's so private she'd never do that, especially not with someone she barely knows."

That was the one piece of good news Zane needed to hear. Now he could breathe more easily again.

Jarod stared at him with his piercing black eyes. "For all the obvious reasons, everyone's thankful you're back for good. Sadie and Ryan have missed you more than you know. And between you and me, we need more law enforcement around here considering all the artifact thefts.

"As Sadie said, there's nothing like knowing a special agent is going to be on the premises from now on. I agree. Welcome home. You make a great addition to the family." He clapped Zane on the shoulder before climbing in behind the wheel.

Zane watched them drive off before he said goodnight to Connor and Liz. They were taking Ralph home. "You can count on me helping you guys with the big move into your new house on Saturday." With all the family pitching in, Avery would have to be there. "I don't have to be on official duty until Monday. That'll give me time to do the things I want and settle in."

Connor's brown eyes lit up. "You're on. You have no idea how good it is to see you and know you're not leaving again."

With everyone gone he walked back into the house. Millie was cleaning up the kitchen while Matt straightened the living room.

"You two go on home. I'll finish up. I can't thank you enough for throwing this party together. It meant the world to me."

Matt was all smiles. "We wanted to do this for you."

"Tell you what. In the morning I'm having breakfast with Jarod and his family. Afterward I'll saddle up Striker and join you at the pasture so you can give me my next ranching lesson."

"It'll be a pleasure."

He walked them out, then locked up and headed for the shower. It had been a red-letter day for him and a long drive. He was tired, but when he got in bed, his mind wouldn't shut off. The vision of Avery coming out of the ranch house with the other man holding on to her arm refused to leave him alone.

Eleven o'clock wasn't late. If, as Jarod had inferred, she barely knew the guy, Zane imagined she might not be home for a long time while they took the time to get better acquainted. A man had to be blind not to be attracted to her.

Whatever was going on between them, Zane wanted to block it from his mind. It had been bad enough all these months while he'd wondered about her. But to actually see her with another guy had set his teeth on edge. Sensing that sleep would be a long time in coming, he got up and went into the den.

He hadn't had a chance to check his email yet. There were four messages. One was sent from Ken, the field manager in Glasgow, who said he was sorry to see him go and wished him the best.

The second one came from Margaret Rogers, a ranger in Glasgow who was great at her job. They'd had dinner half a dozen times over the past year when they'd been out on a case. Wondering what she wanted, he opened her message.

I can't believe you've been transferred! I got in to the office this afternoon and learned you'd been reassigned. Just like that you're gone!

What a shock. You're a cool one, Zane Lawson. I was hoping you'd stick around for a long time, but Ken told me you always wanted to transfer to the Billings office. I didn't know that. What has Billings got that we don't? Don't you know it's a hot spot for criminal activity of the Indian artifacts kind? One of my out-of-state sources says there's a mole in the BIA linked to problems in the Montana sector. Watch your back.

That news didn't surprise him. Zane appreciated the information, but he let out a relieved sigh that his transfer had come before he'd been forced to tell Margaret that he wasn't interested in her. Though, when he'd never asked her out, she had to have known a relationship between them was hopeless, but she was an excellent ranger he trusted.

He replied to her message. In answer to your question, I've come home to the people I love and have missed. You're a fine ranger. Thanks for the heads-up. I wish you the best of luck in the future. Ranger Lawson.

The last two came from Sanders in Billings. He'd enclosed several case files for Zane to study and had marked them top priority. They had to do with vandalism and thefts at several Crow archaeological sites. Margaret had been right on the mark. The information forwarded to the bureau by the local police was fairly detailed. Sanders had charged Zane to find the culprits and arrest them.

He gave the first one a cursory glance. It involved a tepee ring site that had been desecrated. Scanning the second one, the name *Absarokee* leaped out at him. That was the town where Avery was doing her most recent work. Sadie had kept him up-to-date on everyone in both families. He read the background information with renewed interest.

For nearly a decade between 1875 and 1884, the Crow Indian Reservation was located on East Rosebud Creek south of the present-day town of Absarokee, Montana. Population 1,200. Although the tribe moved farther east in 1884, the nine years of living at Absarokee were times of monumental change for the Crow people.

The launch of a road improvement project for Montana Highway 78, which runs through the Crow Indian Reservation's historic Absarokee site, was the impetus for a major archaeological data recovery investigation by the Federal Highway Administration and the Montana Department of Transportation in consultation and cooperation with the Crow Nation.

The team used geographical plotting software to translate the results into a map. The findings revealed the likely presence of artifacts. This area was a transitional point in the history and culture of the Apsaalooké people, thus making it a critical site for their people.

A year in advance of MDT's planned highway reconstruction, a data recovery excavation within the right-of-way limits and on adjacent private land has uncovered significant information, including thousands of artifacts that reveal glimpses into the everyday life of the Crow people more than a century ago.

Avery was intimately associated with this project. She would have invaluable information about the handpicked crew assembled to excavate sacred Crow ground. Things couldn't be working out better. He was jubilant to be armed with a legitimate plan to get close to her through his first case. Tomorrow couldn't get here soon enough. He turned off the computer and wandered through the house to the bedroom he'd turned into a nursery for Ryan.

Now that his nephew was growing up, Zane needed to buy him some new toys for when he slept over. He wanted to take him shopping for some outfits. He ached for children of his own. To Zane, the greatest tragedy in his failed marriage was the fact that Nedra lost interest in having children.

He'd married her at twenty-three when he was already a SEAL. Though he'd warned her of the pitfalls, she'd begged for the marriage and promised to remain strong and independent when he had to be deployed in a war zone. She had a great job with a pharmaceutical company and promises of rising higher.

They'd mapped out their future. He'd assumed the stability of marriage and a family had been her driving force. Unfortunately, she'd never conceived. The fertility specialist they'd consulted hadn't found anything wrong with either of them. Perhaps the stress of Zane's job had prevented conception. He'd suggested they get therapy to help them, but Nedra wanted none of that.

It wasn't until the bitter end of their marriage that she admitted she'd been on the pill for two years without telling him. Her sin of omission was the biggest shocker for him to face.

When she'd finally admitted what she'd done, he'd reached the breaking point. With that hope gone, there was nothing more to fight for. Clearly she'd wanted out of the marriage with no pregnancy issues so she could have fun and excitement with the new man in her life who worked nine to five and then came home. She'd met someone at her job who was going places.

But that was old baggage. After turning out the light, Zane went back to his bedroom. At this point he was in a new phase of his life. He'd had a year to think about it and planned to reach out for what he wanted. Zane wasn't twenty-three anymore, a time when he'd worried that getting married might be a mistake while he was in the SEALs.

This time he knew exactly what he wanted. *He knew the woman he wanted.* Zane had glimpsed Avery from a distance tonight. He was still sizzling from the bolt of electricity that had traveled through him at the sight of her in that green shirt and jeans.

Tomorrow he planned to seek her out, and would use official business as the reason he wanted to talk to her. It was a springboard to the relationship he intended to have with her. One day soon he would find out why she did her best to avoid being alone with him. He knew in his gut there was chemistry between them that was growing stronger every time they saw each other. You could hide a lot of things, but not the kind of sensual tension that picked up on every breath and heartbeat.

Chapter Three

Friday morning Avery got up early and dressed in jeans and a fresh holster shirt. Over it she wore a short-sleeved blue denim Western shirt. In case of an emergency, the snaps made it easier to access her pistol without tearing her shirt.

She slipped out of the ranch house without eating breakfast. Normally she ate with her grandfather, but this morning she was in a hurry and didn't want to hear the news about last night's welcome-home party for Zane. It would hurt too much to know what she'd missed. Pretty soon Ralph would inquire about her date. That was something she would just as soon forget.

She started up her truck and took off for the shooting range outside White Lodge where she put in a half hour's target practice, but last night's events still haunted her. Avery hadn't liked hurting Mike, but she'd had no choice and told him the truth: the man she'd thought she could forget had come back into her life unexpectedly. Though she didn't know what would come of it—maybe nothing—she knew it wasn't fair to use Mike. That was a terrible thing to do to anyone.

Naturally she'd mentioned no name, so Mike couldn't possibly know about her feelings for Zane, who'd been away for close to a year and had only come home periodically. But it was painful how stone-cold quiet Mike had gone on the drive home. Who could blame him? When they reached the ranch house, she'd jumped out of the truck before he could come around. "I'm truly sorry, Mike. Thank you for dinner. Please forgive me."

By the time she made it to the porch, he'd peeled out of the driveway. She could hear the screech of tires even after she'd let herself in the house. The unpleasant moment, compounded by guilt of another kind she'd been carrying around for eight years, had made her sleep fitful.

After picking up a snack, she headed for Little Big Horn College in the town of Crow Agency, Montana. The two-year community college chartered by the Crow Nation offered eight associate of arts degrees. Though the majority of the students enrolled were members of the Crow Nation, it was a public college and she'd been enrolled in Crow language classes on Fridays for a long time.

The hour and a half drive from the ranch put limits on her time so that she could only attend classes once a week. It would take years to achieve any kind of mastery, but she'd always had extra help from Jarod and his Crow family. While she'd been away at college in Bozeman she'd hired a tutor to keep teaching her the language. Because of that ability, she'd won a fellowship to Berkeley.

If she hoped to publish important works in the future, it was vital she be able to communicate with the elderly Crow people on the reservation who could help her with her folklore research. This was her focus, the only thing that was going to help her keep her distance from Zane.

After three hours of classwork, she grabbed a sandwich, left campus and headed for Absarokee. Near the town was an archaeological site that was the former site of Crow Agency along Highway 78. She was part of a crew uncovering part of the foundation of the original agency compound. They'd been compiling a growing collection of artifacts.

She'd found a blue bottle, the ceramic arm of a doll, a pottery shard and the cylinder of a cap-and-ball revolver. The fantastically rich artifact record and archaeologically intact nature of the site made it unique on the high plains of Montana. Actual objects used by the Crow formed a bridge between the past and present. Every piece of evidence excited her because the site was a window into a very transformative time in Crow Nation history.

By midafternoon she pulled up next to some other trucks parked in a field near the ongoing excavation of the foundation of a Crow cabin building that was over a hundred years old. Some kind of meeting was in progress. Paul Osgood, the auburn haired fiftyish professor who headed the dig, waved her over to him and four other archaeologists.

"Hi. What's going on?"

"We're glad you're here. As you can see, vandals

were busy again during the night. I called the police yesterday. They'll do what they can, but it isn't possible for them to patrol this area all the time. They don't have the manpower. Last night someone desecrated part of this foundation we'd marked and tagged into units. The loss of animal and fish bone fragments comes as a real blow."

When Avery looked down, she could see what he meant. The fragments told so much about the changing Crow diet: how they went from living on bison, antelope, deer, elk and cutthroat trout to subsisting on government-provided beef.

"Do you think this is a case of pure and simple looting out of greed? Or malicious vandalism by a bunch of out-of-control teenagers?"

"I have no idea."

"We need a guard dog," she muttered.

"I agree. Unfortunately the benefactors who've funded this project aren't about to give us more money for protection like that."

Ed Meese spoke up. "I could camp out here tonight."

"Not alone," Paul exclaimed.

Ray Collins volunteered to keep watch with him.

Paul shook his head. "I can't allow you to do that. For one thing, it could be dangerous. You don't know what you could be dealing with. I promised the authorities we'd let them handle this, but I've been asked to get some pictures proving the damage. Why don't we walk around the site and take photos of anything we find disturbed? We'll send them to the police and call it a night."

They worked together till six before disbanding. Avery drove back to the ranch totally frustrated by the damage done. For the culprits, it was like taking candy from a baby. Her crew was helpless in the face of the wanton destruction happening after dark.

She pulled in at seven, heartsick over the situation. Avery was just about to pull the key from the ignition when someone walked up to her truck.

Suddenly her heart had another problem. *Zane.*

Avery had been so upset, she hadn't noticed his Volvo sitting next to some of the other vehicles. He was dressed in a dark gray pullover and jeans. His hard-muscled physique standing in cowboy boots made him a good six-three. Between dark fringed lashes, his intelligent eyes glowed like twin blue suns.

With shaky fingers she lowered the window. Now if she could just catch her breath. "I understand congratulations are in order for a lot of reasons. Welcome home. You didn't have to wait until the Fourth of July after all."

A ghost of a smile hovered around his mouth. "Even better, I'm here to stay. You missed a great party last night."

"I'm sorry about that."

He raked a suntanned hand through hair that looked like rich brown loam. "Do you have another date tonight with the same man as last night?"

She blinked. "How did you know about that?"

"I saw the two of you together while I was driving in from Glasgow."

Avery couldn't believe it. She'd been so upset with

herself for having made a second date with Mike, she hadn't been aware of anything else. Biting her lip she said, "I have no plans for tonight. It's been a long day."

"Too long to go out on a case with me tonight? The police alerted the BLM law enforcement to a new problem in the area."

Her head flew back, causing the hair to resettle around her shoulders. "What do you mean?"

"Now that I'm permanently stationed here, my first undercover assignment is to catch the vandals desecrating the dig site at Absarokee."

A small cry escaped her throat. "That's where I work!"

"Sadie told me." He cocked his dark head. "After all these months of working at opposite ends of the state, imagine my surprise. When I saw my orders, it reminded me of a poem that says, 'God long ago drew a circle in the sand exactly around the spot where you are standing right now. I was never not coming here. This was never not going to happen.'"

The words, and the way he'd said them, sounded like bits of prophecy, making their way to her soul where she'd tried to hide from him. She averted her eyes.

"I need someone to give me inside information. Who better than you? Tonight I want to drive there and get a feel for the place. We won't stay too long. If you'll come with me, I'll feed you. While we drive, I'd like to pick your brain."

She cleared her throat, trying to keep her wits about her. "You think someone I work with could be responsible?"

His eyes narrowed, sending a shiver down her back. "You never know. Everyone is fair game at a crime scene."

Zane was on the hunt. She could feel it and shuddered for the people responsible when he caught up with them. "You're right."

"If we leave now in my car, we should get there before it's totally dark."

Avery couldn't very well say no to him under the circumstances. Her truck engine was still idling. "I'll run inside and tell Grandpa where I'm going."

"Good. I'll wait for you."

She raised the window and turned off the ignition. He opened the door so she could climb out. On a burst of adrenaline she hurried into the house only to find out her grandfather had gone over to Jarod's for dinner. She told the housekeeper where she was going, then made a stop to the bathroom to freshen up. While she ran a brush through her hair and reapplied her lipstick, his words kept going around in her head.

I was never not coming here. This was never not going to happen.

ZANE PULLED INTO THE drive-through in White Lodge where they ordered hamburgers and fries. During the short drive from the ranch they talked about family and how big Ryan was getting. She asked about some of his cases in Glasgow. They stuck to topics he knew made her feel comfortable.

Once they were headed for the dig site, he listened while she gave him a rundown of the professors and

archaeologists involved in the excavation. He learned
that two of the men had volunteered to stand guard,
but their idea was tabled by the head archaeologist.

After they arrived, he drove to two of the homes of
the owners of the land to introduce himself and Avery.
He let them know he was conducting an investigation of the vandalism. They received him warmly and
promised to keep an eye out that night. If they saw or
heard anything out of the ordinary, they'd phone him.

Back in the car he said, "Now show me where you
all park when you come to work. Does everyone come
by car?"

"Some have trucks."

Avery gave directions to the part of the field where
they'd been excavating the foundation of a hundred-
plus-year-old Crow cabin. Careful to park where he
wouldn't drive over tracks already made in the dirt,
they got out.

"The worst of the destruction is right over here."
Both of them held flashlights as he followed Avery
to the area set off in grids. "See there? They've raked
through the dirt, destroying the bits of animal bones.
And look here—they've stolen the wire-wound round
glass beads. The beads' eyes, in particular, make them
priceless."

He grimaced. "Stay right here. I'm going to the car
to get some packs of fiber foam." He'd decided not to
cast the tracks. That process was messier. "I want to
take impressions of the tire tracks." One set of them
came from an ATV. He pulled on gloves. "With the
list of names and addresses you're going to give me,

I'll have a better idea of who's driving what. We'll go from there."

"What'll happen when you catch this person?"

"If it's a first offense, we'll levy a twenty-thousand-dollar fine and nine months' jail time. If they've been arrested before, they could be charged a hundred-thousand-dollar fine and get a five-year prison sentence."

"Good! How dare they do this."

Zane smiled at her vehemence. While he gathered evidence, he noticed some cigarette butts. "Does any of your crew smoke?"

"Maybe, but they don't do it on the site."

Interesting.

By ten o'clock he'd gathered the evidence he needed, including the butts and a peppermint pattie candy wrapper he'd found and bagged. Avery helped him carry everything to the car where he discarded the gloves. They started back to the ranch.

He looked over at her. "You're a great helper. When we crack this case, you'll be given a commendation from the Crow Nation, probably by Jarod's uncle Charlo himself. He might as well be your uncle, too, right?"

He provoked a small smile from her. "That's true, but this isn't Crow land."

"It used to be, and the tribe has united with the Federal Highway Administration and the Montana Department of Transportation to make certain this land is preserved."

"Zane, the crew will be really glad to know you've been assigned here."

He felt his pulse surge. "I hope that means you're glad, too, because I'd like to enlist more of your help for this case."

She stirred in the seat. "I'll do anything I can. What they've done is not only criminal, but immoral."

"How about coming over to the house tomorrow after we help Liz and Connor move into their new place? We'll combine forces and get all the information entered in my files."

If he wasn't mistaken, her voice sounded a trifle unsteady as she said, "All right."

Inch by inch, Lawson.

"I understand Connor has a ton of stuff stored at your ranch."

Avery let out a gentle laugh. "You wouldn't believe it. It'll take hours just to transport all his trophies and awards."

Zane grinned. "Then we've got our work cut out." He hoped there'd be so much work, she wouldn't be able to find an excuse to get away from him.

Once he'd pulled up to her ranch, he got out and walked her to the front door. He smiled down at her. In the faint light from the hallway, the classic planes of her features stood out. Between her fantastic coloring and the flare of her mouth, he could hardly tear his eyes away, but he had to. Something strange had happened when he'd looked at her just now.

Everything had been fine all evening, yet all of a sudden she was starting to pull away from him again.

Almost as if he'd pressed a button by mistake and it had opened a secret panel. It wasn't anything she did physically. Rather he felt her emotional withdrawal into that secret opening.

Puzzled by it, he said, "I liked taking you out on this case with me, especially one that impacts you personally. I'm going to bring it to a close soon."

"I don't doubt it. Good night, Zane."

"I'll be over in the morning in my truck and we'll get the move done fast so we'll have more time to devote to the case. The bureau wants to see it wrapped up in a hurry."

She only nodded before slipping inside to shut the door.

He'd seen guys behave the same way after they'd retired from the SEALs. Their PTSD triggered flashbacks and attacks of nerves. Zane still struggled from a mild form of it. He saw a doctor in Billings periodically and was given medication that controlled it. But he'd learned enough about it to know it was a real illness and one not associated only with war.

You could get it after living through or seeing a dangerous event like a hurricane or a bad accident. PTSD made you feel stressed and afraid long after the danger was over. It affected your life and the people around you. Avery exhibited certain signs that led him to believe she might be suffering from it. What in the hell had happened to her to bring it on?

With his emotions in turmoil, he drove home and got ready for bed. His thoughts went back to the night Ned Bannock, Sadie's cousin, had attacked Sadie in

the barn while Zane had been in the house with Ryan.
Thankfully both Connor and Jarod had caught him
in time.

Ned, whose family had always lived on Bannock
property, was still being treated at a mental health facility with occasional supervised visits home. Was it
possible that sometime in the past he'd attacked Avery
and no one ever knew about it?

Had she been too young and frightened to say anything? Had he threatened her to keep quiet? Was that
the reason she'd gone away to college and lost herself
in her work, never letting anyone get too close to her?
Except to be with Ralph, she didn't spend a lot of time
on the ranch. Far from it.

Suddenly something Jarod had said last night gave
him pause. When Zane had suggested she bring her
date to the party, Jarod had given him the oddest stare.
*Avery's so private she'd never do that, especially not
with someone she barely knows.*

What was it Jarod knew? His parting comment to
Zane stood out in red letters.

*Between you and me, we need more law enforce-
ment around here... As Sadie said, there's nothing like
knowing a special agent is going to be on the premises from now on.*

Had Jarod been trying to tell Zane something? The
very thought of a crime being committed against Avery
caused him to break out in a cold sweat. Sleep didn't
come for hours.

WHEN MORNING ARRIVED Zane fixed himself some ce-
real before driving over to the Bannock ranch house

in his truck. The whole family was there pitching in. It was an exciting day for Connor and Liz. Zane had to keep up a cheerful front, but inside his guts were twisted by what he suspected had happened to Avery.

She said hi to him along with the girls, but her eyes didn't linger on him. He had the opposite problem. Today she was dressed in another Western shirt with jeans, this time in chocolate brown. She wore those snap-up shirts like a uniform, but with her shapely figure, he wasn't complaining.

While they carefully wrapped the trophies and smaller items and put them in boxes, he helped the guys carry the boxes and newly delivered furniture to the trucks. The steer wrestler and the barrel racer had built a wonderful modern ranch home with lots of spacious windows to let in the light.

Jarod unboxed a new easy chair so Ralph could sit and watch. The girls came with food. While Zane talked business with Connor for a few minutes, the women stocked the fridge and the cupboards with little Ryan's help.

When Jarod announced there was one more item he needed to bring from his own ranch house, Zane volunteered to drive him so they could talk. The new display case was Jarod and Sadie's housewarming gift. The love between Jarod and Connor reminded Zane of the love he and his big brother, Tim, had shared.

Once they'd loaded it in Zane's truck, he got behind the wheel. But when Jarod slipped inside, Zane didn't start the engine right away. Those black eyes studied him for a minute. "What's on your mind? I can tell there's something."

"I'm afraid so. It kept me awake all of last night." There was only one way to talk with Jarod. Straight and to the point, even if it turned out to be painful.

"You probably don't need your visionary powers to know I've been interested in your sister since I first laid eyes on her. You're her big brother. Now that I'm back for good, I want to pursue a relationship…unless you know something I should know that would stop me before I make a big mistake. Part of me believes she might be interested in me, too."

Jarod took his time answering. "I don't believe you're wrong."

That was a huge admission coming from Jarod. It meant he trusted Zane and that meant everything to him.

"Thank you for your honesty. Just so you know, last night I took her with me to the site at Absarokee to investigate the vandalism."

"She went with you?" He sounded surprised.

"Yes and we got along fine, but when I brought her back, she went into her shell, the kind that's impenetrable. She's done that every time we've been together over the past year. You get so far, then you can't go any further."

Jarod's sudden stillness was the first clue that Zane had hit a nerve.

"I have a theory that she's suffering from a traumatic experience of some kind."

"You're right," Jarod spoke right up, surprising him.

"When I told Uncle Charlo I was worried about Avery, he said that her spirit was imprisoned. That didn't help me at the time. But talking to you about this *does*."

His words gave Zane goose bumps. "Then having said this much, I need to ask you an important question."

Now it was Jarod's turn to appear impenetrable.

"If I've crossed a line and you want me to stop talking, just tell me and I won't bother you with this again."

In the next instant Jarod shifted in the seat so his back rested against the door. Their eyes met in recognition that this was no idle conversation. "You want the truth? I'm thankful Connor and I aren't the only ones who've grown alarmed by her behavior."

Zane let out an anguished sigh. "I'm thankful you just said that."

Jarod leaned forward. "You have a theory?"

He nodded. "Several come to mind."

"One of them being Ned, of course," Jarod stated without hesitation.

"Yes. After what he tried to do to Sadie, it makes you wonder if he ever attacked Avery when she was younger. If she never got help and counseling, it could explain her emotional state now."

His black brows knit together. "The possibility that he'd gotten to Avery long before he attacked Sadie has been a nightmare of mine and Connor's. She's practically stopped dating since she came home from Berkeley. The date with the BIA guy was her first in ages. Her lack of interest in dating is abnormal. We know she's not interested in women, so…" He didn't need to finish the thought.

Zane sucked in his breath. "Let me offer a second possibility. I'm stretching now and it may be farfetched, but do you think she could've been diagnosed with a fatal illness years ago? One that would only give her a certain amount of time to live?"

Jarod's face blanched. They were on frightening territory now.

"If your sister has a death sentence hanging over her head, it might explain her refusal to get involved with anyone. She knows that if your grandfather knew of her condition, it would shatter him or worse."

A mournful sound came out of Jarod. "If that's true, then she's been seeing a doctor nobody knows about and has hidden every symptom of what's wrong except her avoidance of men. I'm more inclined to believe our first theory."

Zane nodded. "A traumatic experience. The doctor I see in Billings would probably diagnose her with PTSD. You don't have to have been in battle to get it. Is she ever around Ned when he comes to the ranch for supervised visits?"

"No. But that's because Ned is only supposed to be with members of his immediate family, not the cousins and extended family."

"Does Avery know what Ned tried to do to Sadie?"

"Yes. Sadie told her."

"Did Sadie notice any kind of reaction in Avery that didn't seem normal?"

"No. I asked her about that. All she saw was Avery's compassion."

"If Ned had done something to her, why wouldn't she have come forward at the time with what she knew to strengthen the case against him? I guess it's possible fear and shame, even a threat, kept her silent."

Jarod stirred in the seat. "Connor and I talk about this all the time. He started noticing changes in Avery when she first went away to college in Bozeman. She seemed fine at the time she left, but when she came home three months later for a visit, she acted different. None of us could put our finger on it. Our grandfather noticed it, too, as if she'd drawn a boundary around herself. You could only come so close."

"She's done that with me since we met," Zane mused aloud. "According to you it was eight years ago that you first started to notice a change in her. She was nineteen?"

Jarod nodded.

"Maybe she was attacked by Ned right before she left the ranch, or else it was someone in Bozeman after she arrived at school. Either way it's clear she's chosen not to tell anyone in your family about it. I wonder if she ever confided in a friend at school."

"I don't know," Jarod muttered. "As far as I could tell she didn't stay in touch with anyone when she came home for visits on weekends. But she's always been close to her cousin Cassie."

"I remember her. Isn't she Ned's younger sister?"

"Yup. She married Logan Dorney, one of our former hands. He had a falling-out with Uncle Grant and is now the foreman over on Sam Rafferty's small hunting ranch east of here. Cassie does a little light housekeeping for Sam. If Avery confided in anyone, it would probably be Cassie."

Zane rubbed his lower lip with his thumb. "I'll keep that in mind. For selfish reasons I've got to find out what's happened to her."

"I'll do everything on my part to help."

Both of them sat there haunted until it dawned on Zane they'd been gone too long. "We need to get back." After starting the engine they took off for Connor's new house.

He looked over at Jarod. "I'm indebted to you for being frank with me. I care about Avery. Today she's going to work on the vandalism case with me. Over time I'm hoping she'll learn to trust me enough to talk to me about what's going on inside her. It isn't natural for such a beautiful, loving woman to have been emotionally locked up like this all these years."

As they got closer to the other house, Jarod let out a groan. "I'm counting on you, Zane. If we find out she was attacked by a pervert who's still on the loose, then I won't rest or spare any resources until we find him and prosecute him to the full extent of the law."

Zane was way ahead of him. "Amen to that. I've got a few ideas to get her to talk to me, but what concerns me most at the moment is that Avery needs to get into counseling if she's ever going to be a whole person again."

"You're right. My sister is Grandpa's little darlin'. She's his biggest worry now."

"I think it's safe to say we're all worried about her," Zane said. "While I'm investigating this new case, I'll keep working on her to open up. I know you will, too. As Sadie has said many times, Avery worships you."

Jarod remained silent after that.

When they pulled up to the new house, it occurred to Zane that maybe her worship of Jarod was the reason she couldn't talk to her big brother. Not if the shame she felt over what had happened to her was too great. Shame was often the by-product of an assault.

But *had* she been assaulted? How many explanations could there be for her behavior? He went over his conversation with Jarod. If she had been diagnosed with a disease that could bring an early death, it could be the reason she refused to get close to any man, knowing she didn't have a lot of time left.

The thought that she could be dying tore him to shreds. He'd had a plan to find out what was wrong, but maybe they were running out of time and he needed to speed up the process.

Together he and Jarod unloaded the display case and carried it into the house. Connor and Liz were thrilled with the gift. While everyone gathered around to help unload the rest of the boxes, he sought out Avery who was in the kitchen doing dishes.

Zane had to restrain himself from grasping her around the waist and pulling her against him. Instead he finished off the rest of the chips and guacamole in one of the bowls sitting on the counter and handed it to her to wash. Then he reached for a dish towel and started drying the dishes.

She glanced at him out of those dark fringed dove-gray eyes. "Thank you, but you don't have to help me."

"I'm highly motivated for us to get busy on the vandalism case. Aren't you?"

She bit the underside of her lip. "You know I am."

His eyes played over her. "Just think. Hundreds of years from now, some archaeologists will excavate this place and find parts of these bowls. One of them will ask, 'I wonder what they ate from these?' The other one will answer, 'Isn't this seed we just found from the avocado family?'"

Laughter pealed out of Avery, bringing her to life. "You're amazing, you know that?"

He hoped so. In fact he hoped he was so amazing she wouldn't be able to live without him.

Chapter Four

Zane asked Avery to follow him through his house to the den. "If you'll give me the phone numbers of your crew, I'll send them to the bureau where they'll pull up names and addresses and any background information for analysis."

She brought up the contact numbers on her cell phone and gave them to him. "Some of the crew have come from universities out of state but decided to work with Professor Osgood for this special project."

When they were done, he got up from the swivel chair. "I need to drive to Billings. There's an express mail facility at the airport. Come with me while I ship the evidence bags and molds overnight to the state crime lab in Missoula. Afterward we'll run by the site to see if any more damage was done during the night. I'll need your eagle eye to know if there's been further desecration."

Her heart pounded like a jackhammer from being with him again like this. She was taking a huge chance going along with him. When he didn't need her assistance anymore, she would have to stop seeing him, but until then she couldn't seem to help herself from falling in with his wishes.

They left his place in the Volvo under blue skies dotted with puffy white clouds. The day was so gorgeous, it hurt. But it wasn't just the weather and the season. She had to admit it was Zane Lawson's presence that filled her with a sense of happiness and well-being she'd forgotten existed.

"I take it the owners you talked to last night haven't called."

"No. I really didn't expect them to. Whoever these culprits are, they'll probably wait a while before making another move. When that happens, I'll be ready for them. Does your crew ever work on weekends?"

"Not that I'm aware of."

He darted a glance at her. "I'm curious. Did you always want to be an archaeologist?"

"Not at first. Jarod got me interested in the Crow culture when he took me out to the reservation. I loved their stories and their ways. I guess I was always fascinated. When he spoke Crow with his family, I wanted to do the same thing so I started taking lessons. I learned that Crow is a Siouan language. By the time I was ready for college, I decided to learn about the Plains Indians. One thing led to another and before long I was hooked."

"That was in Bozeman?"

"Yes."

"Did you live in an apartment?"

Why did he ask her that? Her hands went clammy. "No. A residence hall with several female roommates."

"How did that work out for you?"

She realized he was just making conversation. If only her heart would stop pounding. "Fine."

"I had roommates in the SEALs. They saved my life on many an occasion."

Dr. Moser had advised her to stick with those roommates for emotional and physical safety while she dealt with her trauma. They'd turned out to save her life, too. But she wanted to get off the subject. "Did you love your life as a SEAL?"

"*Love* is an odd word. I enjoyed it and found the life stimulating, but you're living at a high level of intensity all the time. I prefer the life I'm living now."

"Supersleuth without burning all cylinders at the same time."

His chuckle wound its way through her. "Something like that. And I love the scenery."

He stared at her as he said it.

Avery felt as if she was suffocating. This hadn't been a good idea, but she couldn't ask him to take her back home. "Your divorce must have been very hard."

"Not at all. What was hard was finding out Nedra had a lover and wasn't committed to me or the marriage. I kept hoping for children and discovered she'd been on the pill part of the time without telling me."

"Zane—" she said, shock in her tone.

"That was the hard part. When the time came, it was easy to walk away. I've never looked back. Sadie needed help with Ryan. I was glad to leave San Francisco and be able to support her and my nephew. Sadie had always longed for the ranch. When we got here, I could see why she and Eileen had loved it so much."

Avery hadn't known all this about him. He'd lived through a lot of pain. "I've never seen anyone fit in so fast. Matt says you're a natural at ranching."

He grinned. "Since I hired him, he has to say that, doesn't he? Even though I know next to nothing about the difference between heifers and cows."

Her eyes smiled at him. "The point is, you're a quick study. When he says something he means it, so you should feel complimented. You should have seen Connor's first wife, Reva. She couldn't stand ranch life. It tore my brother up for a long time."

"Obviously ranching isn't for everyone and not every marriage takes no matter how hard you try. I'd say Connor hit the jackpot with Liz."

"Grandpa always said they were two peas in a pod, but neither of them knew it until they went to finals together."

"Your family has found paradise here. I figure if I'd come out to Montana in the late 1800s, I would have bought up a piece of land right around here the way your great-great-grandfather did. But it doesn't matter if I'm a hundred and twenty years late because I'm here now and not going anywhere."

"I'm happy for you, Zane."

"So what about you?" The questions kept coming. "Is the man you were with the other night someone important to you?"

She angled her head away from him. "No."

"How many men have there been in that long string

of hopefuls who asked you to marry them? Don't tell me there weren't any because I wouldn't believe you."

She was starting to feel sick. *Please no more personal questions.* "To marry? Not many." Blaine Robertson's proposal in high school was the only one. Ben, their family's former foreman had hinted at it. "What about you? Have you met anyone since your divorce who tempted you to marry again?"

"One woman has captured my attention, but these are early days yet."

Her heart plunged to her feet and she wasn't even standing. "You're a mentally healthy man to be able to say that after what you've lived through."

"If you mean I haven't lost the ability to trust after what my wife did to me, you'd be right. But the fact is, not everything was her fault. Before we married I questioned if it was a good idea or not. Being married to someone in the military and making the marriage work takes extra dedication. I went into our marriage with doubts. That alone should have told me not to do it."

"You're an honest man, too. You remind me of Connor. He said that when he married Reva there was a part of him that feared she'd never be able to take to ranching. It turned out he was right."

"Yet we learn from our mistakes. I know I'll never make the same one again," he vowed in his deep voice. "Look at Connor now. Second time around he found the perfect woman for him."

Avery was still struggling with what he'd told her. With the air frozen in her lungs, she turned to look blindly out the passenger window. They'd already reached the airport. She sat there in physical and emotional pain while he went inside to ship the evidence he'd gathered. He came back out with a smile before she'd had time to think.

"I'm glad we're going to see the site in broad daylight. I'm curious to find out if there's been more damage. That's where you can help me. It's easy to miss clues in the dark. Is there anything you need before we leave town?"

"No, but thank you for asking."

Zane drove fast, totally unaware of what his admission about a woman he had his eye on had done to Avery. While they headed for Absarokee, he spoke about the desecration of some tepee rings in the Pryors he needed to investigate. Clearly he didn't intend to talk anymore about his romantic leanings. She couldn't have handled it if he'd said another word.

Avery was glad she didn't know more. All this time she'd been secretly pining for Zane, he'd been interested in someone else. Wait till she told Dr. Moser. Now the burden of ever having to tell Zane her secret could stay buried.

One thing was certain. She planned to move to the reservation soon. Her grandfather wouldn't like it, but she would need to do it for a total separation from the past.

"That's quite a conversation you're having with yourself." Zane's comment brought her back to the here and now. They'd been walking around the site. No one from the crew was there. The field looked deserted.

"Sorry. I was thinking about the people who did this destruction."

"There've been too many of them over the years nationwide. With tens of thousands of Indian sites in North America alone, thieves have had a field day." After they'd visited each excavated spot, he turned to her. "What do you think?"

"Nothing more seems disturbed."

"I agree."

"Do you think they'll come back?"

"That's hard to say. Let's head for White Lodge and have dinner before we go home."

Now that she knew Zane's interest in her was only platonic, she felt wooden inside. Though she couldn't believe it, evidently all the vibes she'd felt from him were only her own wishful thinking, which was crazy since she'd been afraid to get close to him. "Good idea. I didn't realize how long we've been gone."

Once again they were on the road. In a few minutes Zane's cell phone rang. He checked the caller ID, but didn't answer.

She eyed him covertly. "I take it that wasn't an emergency."

"I doubt it."

"Even so, it could be important. Why don't you pull over and talk? We're not in a hurry."

"The person phoning me can wait until I call them back."

"Uh-oh. That must mean it's someone from your fan club."

"Come again?"

"Sadie says you leave women in the dust all the time and don't even know it," she teased. "Connor had the same problem."

He flashed her a beguiling smile. "Let me satisfy your curiosity. It's one of the rangers from Glasgow. I left before she knew I was being transferred. Sometimes she helped me on a stakeout."

"Is she married? Single?"

"Divorced. For a lot of reasons my transfer came at the right time."

"You mean she'd been hoping you'd ask her out."

"Maybe, but I was never interested."

"That doesn't stop a person from hoping."

"She sent me an email yesterday expressing her surprise that I'd already gone. I responded and wished her well. I'll get back to her in a while. Right now I'm with you and I'm enjoying it. You can't imagine how happy I am to be running the office out of my own home."

"After your personal sacrifice in the military, you've certainly earned the right."

"It feels good to be doing what I want at last. I like working alone with the freedom to carry out plans my own way."

"I hear you. Being on a crew at the dig site is only part of what I do. Research takes up most of my time and it's something I can do alone on my own schedule."

"We're lucky to love the work we do," he murmured. They came around the bend. White Lodge lay straight ahead. "Let's go to the Rosebud, shall we? I hear their Saturday night barbecue isn't half-bad."

Avery chuckled to camouflage her torn-up emotions. "Such praise, Agent Lawson."

He pulled into the parking lot. They got out and entered the crowded restaurant. Zane had his name put on the list before walking back to her. "There's a ten-minute wait. Shall we go in the bar on the other side till they call us?"

"Sure."

He ushered her through the crowd with a certain authority that took her breath away. Avery saw the way the women stared at him. He wore a navy blue crewneck sweater and jeans. With his strong, tall build and medium cropped dark brown hair, no male in the whole state of Montana could begin to compare.

Zane found them space at the end of the bar. There was only one stool. With his hand on her back, he urged her to sit. The second she did and turned, she found herself staring straight into the unfriendly black eyes of Mike Durant. *Oh, no.*

Avery couldn't believe he was seated on the stool next to her. He appeared to be alone. Good manners required something of her. She spoke first.

"Hello, Mike." Zane was watching them. "Mike Durant? May I introduce you to a family friend, Zane Lawson."

He nodded to Zane. "I take it you're the guy who's come back to White Lodge."

"That's right. How did you know?"

"Avery mentioned it the other night on our date."

Mike was really angry or he wouldn't have been so bold. She took a quick breath while Zane reached out to shake his hand. "It's nice to meet you. Was that your BIA truck in front of her ranch?"

"Yeah."

"What a coincidence. I saw it before I pulled into my ranch next door. I've been transferred to the Billings BLM Law Enforcement Division. With all the vandalism going on, chances are we'll be bumping into each other from time to time on patrol."

Mike finished his beer. "We probably will. Good night." He gave up his stool. The guy sitting on the other side of him got up, too, and they left together, working their way through the crowd.

Avery felt as if she'd been shoved off a cliff.

Zane took one look at her and said, "We haven't been served yet, so why don't we leave? It's a short drive home."

She didn't need any urging.

"When we get there I'll fix you an omelet even Ryan gobbles down."

Everything Zane said and did was getting to her.

Again she'd been so preoccupied with thoughts of him, she hadn't noticed the BIA truck in the parking lot. All of this could have been avoided. As he walked her to his car, she saw the truck take off down the street going faster than was legal.

On their way home Zane looked at her. "He was angry enough to make you uncomfortable. Why was that?"

"When he brought me home the other night, I told him I couldn't go out with him again. I hated hurting him so I used the excuse that someone I cared about had come back into my life unexpectedly. You can't imagine my shock at seeing him in there."

"That explains why he wanted to flatten me. There was something about him. I felt his negativity. How long has he lived in the area?"

"He was assigned here from Nebraska after the holidays. The elders at Crow Agency are depending on him to help track down the people stealing the artifacts."

"Have you ever seen the guy he was with before?"

"No."

After a moment's reflection he said, "I don't blame him for being upset that I came in with you. Every man in the restaurant would have loved to deck me in order to be with you tonight. Under the circumstances you have to admire his self-control."

"You're good on a woman's ego, Zane."

"Since you used me as your excuse for turning him down, I think we're even."

Heat crept into her face. "Before I went upstairs to get ready that night, Grandpa told me the news about your coming home. It was the first thing that came to mind when faced with my dilemma about telling him I couldn't see him anymore."

"I used you, too, when I replied to Margaret. I told her I'd come home to the people I love and have missed."

Avery's heart nearly failed her to hear him say that. "You've convinced me that ranger has a crush on you."

"You've heard the saying 'out of sight, out of mind,'" he murmured. "Make me a promise, Avery. If Durant comes near you again in a way that makes you at all nervous, I want to know about it."

"I'm sure he won't."

"Sadie wasn't careful enough where Ned was concerned and we know how that turned out. I promised your brothers I'd look after all of you now that I'm back."

When did he tell them that?

She shook her head. "Ned wasn't normal from my first memory of him. It's very sad what happened to him. He did a horrific thing to Jarod and Sadie by keeping them apart all those years ago, but I also have a hard time forgiving him for what he did to Cassie and her husband, even if he is in a mental facility."

"What do you mean?"

"He bad-mouthed Logan to my uncle Grant and told lies about him sleeping with Cassie that weren't true. That's why Uncle Grant told Cassie he fired Logan even though she swore nothing happened and that she loved Logan.

"My uncle was always afraid of Ned. Everyone in their family was. Because of that, Uncle Grant was beyond listening to reason and warned Cassie that if she married Logan, he'd cut her off and she wouldn't be welcome at home anymore."

Zane's body unexpectedly tensed. "Does anyone else know the truth about that story?"

"No, I'm the only one. Because Ned frightened her, she spent most of her time with me to get away from him. It was easy because our houses were so close together on ranch property. We ended up sharing everything."

"Has your uncle made his peace with Cassie and her husband yet?"

"No. Uncle Grant is a mess with so many regrets, he and my aunt are still on shaky ground. He needs counseling."

"I couldn't agree more. Sounds like your cousin Cassie needs it, too."

"Since their family had to go in for a psychiatric evaluation because of Ned, she's getting it now, thank heaven."

"Counseling's a good thing. I know I've needed it."

"You?"

"I didn't get out of the SEALs without some collateral damage."

She stared at him. "You have PTSD?"

"I do, but for the most part I have it under control."

"I didn't know that about you."

He shot her a glance. "Does that alarm you?"

Not when she'd been diagnosed with it herself. "Of course not. Anyone who's lived through war has demons."

"But what if you found yourself in love with someone with PTSD? How do you think you would feel?"

"My heart would go out to him."

"But it wouldn't turn you off or frighten you?"

Was he afraid this woman he was interested in would be afraid? "Not at all."

"That's reassuring to hear because I have a favor to ask."

What?

"After I fix dinner I'll tell you about it." They pulled into his ranch and parked in front under a darkening sky.

"I don't need an omelet, Zane. A peanut butter sandwich will do me just fine. I'll make it."

"You and Connor are a lot alike," he quipped. "While I check my emails, make me one, too. Peanut butter's always been my favorite."

They walked into the house. After she'd freshened up, she entered the kitchen and got out the bread and peanut butter. He joined her and added milk from the fridge. In a minute they sat at his breakfast table to eat.

"What's this favor all about, Zane?"

"I'm going on a stakeout at the site for the next two nights. I'll be gone all day tomorrow, as well. Connor is letting me rent his trailer. I need a partner who's up-to-date on the case and can give me an extra set of eyes and ears." His intense blue gaze fused with hers. "Would you be willing to do the honors?"

Zane wanted her to stay overnight in the trailer with him? Avery was so surprised she stopped chewing. "You mean you're going back there again tonight?"

He nodded. "I'm headed to your ranch soon to hitch up the trailer. If your answer is no, I'll drop you off first."

"Then you think the culprits are coming back?"

His eyes narrowed. "I think they've waited long enough before trying to make another haul of artifacts. As you pointed out, there are a lot more of them still in the ground. The police can't be there every night and they know it. I plan to surprise them if they show up."

"But what about the trailer being in sight?"

"I've obtained permission from one of the land owners to use their right-of-way road to park. Anyone watching will assume the trailer belongs to the owner." He finished off the last sandwich and cleaned up the kitchen. "Excuse me while I pack some things."

Her heart was thudding again as they left the house a few minutes later in his truck. When they pulled into her ranch, he slowed down in front of the ranch house. "What's your decision?"

He wasn't interested in her, but he'd asked for her help in solving this case. Though she knew there would be a price to pay later, more than anything in the world she wanted to go with him, be with him one more time. "I'll come with you. While you hitch up the trailer, I'll hurry inside and pack an overnight bag."

"Good. I'll be back in ten minutes." He stayed where he was so his headlights were trained on her until she let herself in the door.

The first thing she did was hurry down the hall to her grandfather's room. He was still up watching the ten o'clock news.

"There you are!"

"Hi, Grandpa." She kissed him. "I'm back, but I'm leaving again and won't be home until Monday morning."

He took off his glasses. "Where are you going?"

"Zane has asked me to help on a case at the Absarokee site." She explained the details. "We're going to keep watch."

"Well, as long as you're with him, I'm not worried. He'll catch those renegades before long." He didn't even blink about her plans. That was how much he trusted Zane.

"I'll call you tomorrow with an update. Love you."

"You, too, darlin'. Give Zane my best."

"I will."

She rushed through the house and up the stairs to get packed. In a few more minutes she stepped out on the porch with her small suitcase. Zane was waiting in front. He'd driven up with Connor's black-and-silver trailer. Avery felt like a thief sneaking out in the night on some clandestine adventure. Excitement raced through her body.

Zane levered himself from the truck and reached for her case, which he put in the backseat. When he walked around to open the passenger door for her, she climbed in the cab, but their arms and legs brushed. The contact sent a curl of warmth through her body.

"Grandpa sends his regards," she said to counteract her reaction. "You're a favorite of his."

"The feeling's mutual. It comes with the territory of being related to Sadie."

Not necessarily, but Avery didn't voice her thoughts. Ralph Bannock was a shrewd judge of character and no one's fool. He'd been impressed with Zane from the first day.

Zane shut her door and walked around to get in behind the wheel. They took off. "When we get to White

Lodge, we'll stop at the supermarket and pick up some groceries. Whatever sounds good to you. On the drive over, I'd like to hear about this latest book you're writing based on your thesis."

She swung her head around, causing her hair to swish across her shoulders. "Who told you about that?"

"Your brothers. They're open in their praise. Jarod's so proud of you he could burst, but he lets you know in a different way."

Warmth filled her cheeks.

"The reason I know he cares so much is that he recently told me you've honored his mother's people by undertaking this work. The undertones of love were apparent."

Tears smarted her eyes. "Thank you for telling me that. I'm no writer in the sense you mean. What I *am* doing, as you already know, is working on a collection of stories from the Crow culture. They're a compilation of personal narratives, legends, myths and historical traditions.

"My biggest struggle during interviews—that is if I'm granted an interview—is to translate their words correctly in order to preserve their stories with the greatest accuracy. It's a painstaking process and I work with a tape recorder. Sometimes it's overwhelming. You have to understand I'll be studying their language for the rest of my life."

"I'm still working on English," he quipped. "Tell me one of the stories."

She shook her head. "You're just humoring me."

"I asked because I'm fascinated," he came back in

a serious tone. "Part of my job is dealing with the national Safe Indian Community Initiative. I'll be working with the Crow people from time to time for the rest of my life. I need to learn everything I can."

She couldn't help but admire his inquiring mind. "Have you ever heard of the Spirits of the Rivers?"

"No. You'll have to teach me."

"Well, there's one thing you need to understand first. The members of the Crow Nation were animists. In other words, they believed spirits were everywhere in nature. They make the grass and plants grow. They cause the winds to blow and the clouds to float. They believe every animal and bird has a spirit.

"A boy, or a girl in some tribes, wants to partake of this mystery power from nature and spends a few days and nights alone in a place of supernatural power to fast and dream. The spirit of an animal speaks to him in human form, teaching him his individual sacred song. Jarod went for four days and nights on his quest."

"I had no idea."

"He was taught to be patient and believes his dream helped him to wait for Sadie."

"You've just given me goose bumps."

She laughed gently. "I know what you mean. He has the gift of vision like his uncle Charlo. He told Sadie he knew Liz would win the overall barrel racing championship several days before it happened, but he didn't have the same dream for Connor."

A strange sound came from Zane's throat. She could tell she'd grabbed his attention.

"There are several tales of the Spirits of the Rivers in the Crow oral history. From earliest times they say strange animals or spirits have lived in the rivers. They're always hungry and ready to devour humans. I'll tell you one.

"The old woman Red Feather who repeated this story to me was taught by her grandmother to always throw food into the water before crossing it so she would be spared. And she needed to paint her body with spots and stripes in bright colors to frighten the spirits. The last spirit she saw was in the Rosebud River. It had the form of a human, but it was very fat and had unusually small limbs."

Zane turned to her. "And she told you this?" They were coming into White Lodge.

"Absolutely. One day if you like, I'll take you to meet her and translate for you so you'll have heard it from her mouth." That comment had just slipped out, shocking her. There'd be no "one day"...

"She's an entertainer and a historian. Storytelling is an inherent part of her culture. They have a strong oral tradition and do a lot of their storytelling at night in winter with their children gathered round."

He pulled into the supermarket parking lot. "After we get settled in Absarokee for the night, I want to hear all the other river stories."

"You'll fall asleep long before then."

His eyes flashed that brilliant blue. "You want to make a bet?"

Her pulse rate flew off the charts.

Zane took her inside the store with him and they bought what they'd need so they wouldn't have to leave the trailer. Over the past year he'd dreamed of being with her like this and could hardly believe it had become a reality.

He considered it a big breakthrough for her to stay with him in the trailer. Whatever had caused her to tense up on him the other night, he no longer had the feeling she was nervous around him. It seemed that since he'd told her of a woman he was interested in, she'd dropped some of her defenses and was interacting with more warmth and enthusiasm.

But he wouldn't be able to keep up the facade for too much longer before she saw through him. Already he knew a few days and nights without holding and kissing her would never satisfy him. Then the truth of his feelings would have to come out.

Chapter Five

When they reached the dig site, Zane drove the trailer onto the private road past one of the owner's homes. He continued enough of a distance for it to look as if the owner was leaving the trailer there out of the way. Together with Avery they carried everything into the trailer.

She put the food away and closed the fridge. "I can see why Connor said he could have lived in here with Liz on a permanent basis and have been perfectly happy. It has everything a person needs—a living-slash-dining room, kitchen, bathroom, TV..."

"A home on wheels. If you'll plan to sleep in the niche and keep watch through the window you can open, I'll take the sofa pullout bed, so I can come and go quickly from the roof." He handed her a black case.

"What's this?"

"Go ahead and open it."

She put it on the table and did as he asked. The second she lifted the lid, he heard a quiet cry. "Two pairs of night-vision goggles with headgear!" She darted him a natural smile that made her so entrancing it was impossible to look away. "Something left over from your SEAL days?"

"You guessed it. It's amazing what you can see with them, and your hands are free. No spy should be without them."

She chuckled. "You mean you'll trust me with one of these?"

"I thought you understood I brought you along to help me."

Avery did a little jump. "This is going to be fun!" For just a moment she was a different person, acting carefree and happy. He'd do whatever it took to make her this excited all the time.

"Come on. We'll take these outside in the dark and put them on. You'll see green imaging."

She followed him out into the balmy night air and waited while he adjusted the lenses and helped her with the headgear. He longed to plunge his fingers in her hair, but again he had to wait until the time was right.

"I don't believe what I'm seeing," she said softly. "Oh, Zane—"

The breath caught in his lungs to hear her thrilled reaction. "It's pretty amazing the first time you look through them."

"I feel like a superhero with magic powers."

He laughed. "What's even more amazing is when you lock onto a target that comes in range."

"To think you used these all the time in the SEALs," her voice trailed. "It's a miracle you survived what you were sent to do. How bad is your PTSD?"

She sounded as if she really wanted to know. "It's

much better now. Mostly I have bad dreams. Sometimes I wake up disoriented and have night sweats, but the sensation goes away faster than it used to. If I seem agitated, just talk to me calmly and I should be fine. Now, tell me what you see out there."

Her goggles were aimed at the site probably three hundred feet away. "I don't know. I keep looking." While she was engrossed, he was totally engrossed in her. "Oh—there's a rabbit!"

"I don't think he's our culprit."

Soft laughter bubbled out of her. "Hey—I think I see a chipmunk!"

Zane had seen it and the rabbit and half a dozen other small animals. No humans yet. If anyone planned to come, it would probably be around two in the morning.

She moved farther away from the trailer door and looked all around. "I've never had so much fun!" Suddenly she turned toward him and actually jumped. "Wow!"

"Am I really that scary?"

"Yes! Take off your headgear. I want to see what you look like without it."

Smiling, he removed it. "Is this better?"

"Not really. You don't look the same."

"How *do* I look?" He was curious.

"Alien." But she laughed before he realized she was teasing him.

"I hear that some green aliens are pretty good-looking," he teased back.

She removed her headgear. "I've heard some aliens

are good at fishing for compliments. For your information, you don't need to fish. Without the goggles I can understand why Sadie says you leave hordes of females in the dust."

"Hordes?"

"Now that I can see you clearly, I don't think that's an exaggeration. How could your wife have given you up?"

The tremor in Avery's voice touched him in areas he didn't know were there. "She wanted a different life."

"Did she know about your PTSD?"

"We got to a point in our marriage that she didn't care."

Avery looked down. "That's so incredible to me." She started for the door and opened it. Before she stepped inside she turned to him. "But there's something else I find even more incredible."

"What's that?"

"Your PTSD isn't obvious. You handle it in a way that's remarkable."

Zane had trouble swallowing. "I'm glad, if you haven't noticed. But one day you'll catch me out. Something will trigger a flashback and my behavior will be different."

On that note her smile faded. Once again he'd touched on something that had disturbed her. She went inside and put her goggles on the table. "If it's all right with you, I'll use the bathroom first before I climb up to the niche."

"Go ahead." After she disappeared he grabbed a chocolate doughnut and opened his laptop. His first order of business was to send in a report to the Billings office apprising them of the weekend stakeout. No word back from the lab in Missoula yet. To his surprise there was another message from Margaret who had more information. He'd call her later.

He sent a message to Connor thanking him for the use of the trailer. One more message to Sadie and Jarod, letting them know he was with Avery keeping watch over the dig site for the next couple of days. The last message went to Matt and Millie, informing them he'd be back Monday to put in some time on the ranch.

Zane had just finished when Avery emerged from the bathroom. She was still dressed in her clothes and reached for one of the pairs of goggles. She started for the ladder. He got up from the table. After she reached it and started to climb, he put a hand on her back to assist her.

"Don't touch me!" she cried out as if in terror.

But it was too late. In that instant she used a technique on him she had to have been taught in a self-defense class. As she dropped down and used her elbow as a weapon, his hand felt something hard under her top beneath her left arm, and he knew exactly what it was. Pure revelation flowed through him. He could rule out fatal illness as the reason for her behavior.

She'd been assaulted.

Before this minute it had only been speculation on his part, but no longer. The knowledge ripped his guts to pieces. She scrambled into the niche with the goggles. He stood at the bottom of the ladder and looked up at her. "I'm sorry, Avery. I didn't mean to startle you."

"It's all right. I know you were only trying to help. Forgive me."

"I should have realized you don't need it."

In a lightning moment, everything had changed for him. He couldn't touch her the way he wanted to. Getting physically close to Avery would be like navigating through a minefield. You had to deal with the mental component before you did anything else. Even before that, she needed to know how he felt about her in order to lay a groundwork of trust. He'd frightened her, the last thing he'd ever want to do.

"I'm going outside to climb the ladder to the roof. Why don't you open your window? We'll take turns watching. When you get tired, call to me and let me know."

"I will. Same goes for you."

A few minutes later Zane lay down on his sleeping bag on top of the roof, his goggles within reach. In the small holster of his belt was his SIG Sauer 40-caliber gun. He had everything he needed to protect them.

But no one had been there to protect Avery.

During wartime he'd seen a lot of that kind of atrocity from the enemy. He thanked God he'd never known anyone personally who'd undergone such evil trauma. It crushed him to realize that Avery of all people had been a victim and was still suffering acutely.

His eyes filled. He groaned for her and her torment.

Zane had been trained for a lot of contingencies in his life, but there was no training for this. He didn't know which foot to put in front of the other. He needed to talk to his counselor in Billings. He'd drive there early on Monday morning.

Before that he'd drive her back to the ranch tomorrow morning. She needed to be around the safety of her family. Keeping watch from the trailer had been a bad idea. In wanting to be alone with her, he'd learned her secret, but he'd made a grave mistake at the same time.

Now that he knew the truth about her, he found himself hoping the culprits didn't show up tonight. He wanted to get her home without incident and would have to think up a good excuse for their change in plans. It didn't take him long to come up with an idea that wouldn't be a lie, only the timing of it would be since he'd tentatively scheduled it for a few days from now.

It was going to be a long, agonizing night.

AVERY'S QUIET SOBS soaked her pillow. A few minutes ago she'd suffered a flashback. She'd jerked away from his touch like she'd been taught to do in her self-defense class and had offended him deeply. How could she have cried out like that for him to stop when he'd been nothing but wonderful to her? He'd asked about her work and encouraged her to tell her stories. He'd asked for her help on this case. She'd never been so flattered in her life.

Though she wasn't afraid of him, he didn't know that, not after what she'd done. Her reaction had been pure reflex because she feared he might discover she was carrying a handgun. Then he'd want to know why and she wouldn't be able to lie to him with conviction.

For him to know the truth of what had happened to her would kill her.

She could still see those gorgeous blue eyes staring up at her with the most painful expression she'd ever seen. He'd already been so hurt by his wife, by the war, by the death of his brother and parents. He'd told her things about his personal life and had confided in her.

Now *she'd* hurt him and she couldn't stand it. She needed to make it up to him, but how?

For the rest of the night she sat propped by the window and watched for activity. But if Zane called to her, she didn't hear him. When she next became aware of her surroundings, the sun was out and she was slumped in a corner of the bed with the goggles lying at her side. Sorrow engulfed her. She couldn't even keep watch with him through the night.

After closing and locking the window, she moved down the ladder with the goggles. There was no sign of Zane. Once she'd packed them in the case still lying on the table, she freshened up in the bathroom. Her hair needed a good brushing and she could use some lipstick so she wouldn't look so pale.

When she opened the trailer door, she could see him in the distance talking to the home owner. Had he even been to bed? She glanced at her watch. It was eight-thirty. The first thing she needed to do was apologize to him, but he was taking so long to come back she started to get nervous.

They'd bought bagels and cream cheese. She could get out those items and make coffee for when he got back. As she was pouring it into mugs, he walked into the trailer wearing a green pullover and jeans. His five o'clock shadow only enhanced his male appeal. Their eyes met. His troubled gaze searched hers for a fleeting moment.

"Good morning, Avery." His voice sounded an octave lower first thing in the morning.

"Good morning." She put the pot back on the stove. "I'm so sorry I let you down last night," she blurted.

"What do you mean?"

"I didn't help you. I fell asleep and feel awful about it."

"If I'd needed you, I would have woken you up. It turns out we didn't have visitors last night. I've talked to the owner of this field and he's going to do a watch with the other owner tonight, so we can head back to the ranch whenever you're ready."

Avery's stomach scrunched up in renewed pain that he wanted to take her home today. Who could blame him? "Aren't you hungry? I fixed us some breakfast."

"Thank you. It looks delicious." He sat down and ate three bagels and drank two cups of coffee. She was thankful he had an appetite at least.

"Was it the owner's idea or yours about tonight's arrangement?" she asked. "Because if you've decided to leave now instead of waiting until tomorrow, then I know it's my fault."

He flicked her a veiled glance. "I don't know what you're talking about."

"Yes you do, but you're too much of a gentleman to remind me of my bad behavior. We both know I was rude to you last night, but you have to know I didn't mean to be. I feel like such a fool. Please don't change your plans. You made all these arrangements with Connor for the use of the trailer and I really want to stay and help."

"Avery—"

"I know you couldn't have gotten any sleep last night," she broke in on him. "Why don't you go to bed and sleep through the day. I'll sit outside the trailer on one of the loungers and read while I sunbathe. No one's going to come to the field in daylight. Tonight you can be on watch again and I'll sleep. That way the owners don't have to stay up."

He shook his head. "I had every intention of following through with our original plan until I received an email this morning from the Billings office. My boss wants me there at the crack of dawn tomorrow on official business. That's why I'm taking you home now. If I have an early night tonight, I can be up early and make that appointment on time."

Avery didn't believe him, not for a second, but she refused to say or do anything else to offend him. "Of course. Official business has to come first. I'll just clean up the kitchen and we can take off."

They worked together, gathering their things, then left the trailer and got in the truck. Zane started it up and they drove on through the private access road to the other side of the field. Tomorrow she'd be back here again working with the crew. None of them would know what she'd been doing out here with Zane.

All the time she fought tears during the drive home, he told her about the new case that required his presence in Billings. "It seems that vandals have blown up a lot of BLM signs, including the one for the Shepherd Ah Nei Recreation Area. The amount of repairs has escalated to the tune of thirty-thousand dollars."

"That's horrible."

"And the costs are still going up," he said. "It's taking away the recreation fund that has been set up. My boss fears all the vandalism, including that at Absarokee, is related. He's putting a task force together and wants input from the agents. That's why I have to go in tomorrow."

Maybe she'd been wrong and he was telling the truth. Right now she was so devastated by her behavior and confused, she didn't know what to think. "I hope you catch them."

"It's a never ending battle, Avery."

"I know."

He leaned back in the seat. "Until we get back to the ranch, how about entertaining me with another one of your Spirits of the River stories."

Zane was kind to a fault, trying to make good from a bad situation. If she did nothing else, she could play along and try to forget what happened last night.

"One of the men on the reservation named Long Hair told me about three spirits his ancestor saw in the Little Bighorn River. They were creatures who played in the water like children. At first he thought they were children, but they were spirits.

"While he sat on his horse to watch, a flash of lightning lashed the water into foam and dazzled the man. His horse reared in fright and threw him. When he got up, the spirits were gone, but he could follow the track of the flash by a muddy line in the water. The spirits had been in the lake at the head of the Little Bighorn."

Zane darted her a glance. "Every bit of Crow knowledge is useful. I'm indebted to you. Thank you for going out there with me last night. Stakeouts can get lonely. It was enjoyable for me. If I had a partner like you, I wouldn't mind going out on one every night of the week."

"I enjoyed it, too. Especially looking through those goggles. They'd be fun to take on a hike after dark in the Pryors. Wouldn't it be awesome to watch the wild horses running through the gullies? With their manes flowing, there's no more beautiful sight on earth. Imagine them in the moonlight."

"I'll talk to your brothers. We'll have to get a group of us together and do it."

Avery didn't want to be a part of that group if he were to bring someone else along. During the stakeout she'd discovered one unassailable truth. She'd lost her heart so completely to Zane, her life would never be the same again.

MONDAY MORNING ZANE sat in the waiting room on standby status for three hours until Dr. Lindstrom could fit him in. When the nurse finally called his name, a frantic Zane rushed into his office.

"Thank you for fitting me in on your lunch hour. I'll make it worth your time."

"Forget that." The doctor told him to sit down. "Are you suffering from another flashback?"

"No." Zane sat forward with his hands clasped between his legs. "This is something completely different. I'm in love with a woman I met a year ago. I believe she loves me, but she has boundaries I've never been able to cross.

"Because of her behavior I've suspected she has a form of PTSD. By accident I discovered she's carrying a weapon in a holster shirt. It supports my theory that she's been assaulted. Through her family I've learned that she rarely dates. After talking to her brothers, we assume the assault must have happened eight years ago."

"Does she know you know?"

"Not yet. That's why I'm here. Night before last I was helping her up a ladder when she cried out in reaction and did a self-defense move on me she had to have learned from a professional. Before I fell back to give her space, I could feel the weapon under her arm. She apologized for reacting like that but didn't explain."

Restless, Zane made a furrow through his hair. "I'm shattered by the knowledge that she's been violated. To be honest, I'm angry in a way I've never been before. Though I've seen this situation several times during my military career, it didn't impact me personally."

He jumped out of the chair and started pacing. "This is different, Doctor. Personal. I don't know how I'm ever going to get over it. If I feel this way, I can only imagine how she must feel. I don't know how to treat her. I'm here for help."

"Sit down, Zane. We'll take this one step at a time. Violence against a woman changes her life forever. If this happened eight years ago, then she's been living with the consequences for a long time. Tell me about her."

Zane took a deep breath and related what he could.

"She sounds like an intelligent, well-educated, remarkable woman who is coping well on the surface. The fact that she's armed and has learned self-defense techniques means she got help and is probably seeing a therapist."

"I pray to God that's true."

"Am I to understand that no physical intimacy has gone on between the two of you?"

His eyes closed tightly. "None." In the next few minutes Zane explained the circumstances since he'd first come to Montana.

"So what you're saying is, now that you've been transferred to the Billings office, this weekend was the first time you had a chance to get close to her?"

"Yes. I took her with me on a stakeout of the archaeological site where she's been working. It provided the perfect opportunity for us to be together alone. Because she has always been guarded, I knew I had to be careful. Everything went fine until it was time to start our watch.

"I have to tell you, I didn't expect what happened in the trailer when I tried to steady her on the ladder. We would have stayed over one more night, but I decided to take her home yesterday to allay any fear of mine."

The doctor nodded. "That was a good instinct. Let me ask you something. Have you ever indicated before the other night that you're in love with her?"

Zane shook his head. "No. Our families are closely connected so she has known about my divorce since the first day we met. She's learned some things about me and my background from the few times we've been together. But I decided that this stakeout would be the perfect time to let her know how strong my feelings run."

"Were you hoping she might figure out *she* was the woman you'd referred to?"

"Maybe, on a subconscious level. I wanted to build her up first so she'd trust me. I planned to tell her the truth before the stakeout was over, but that incident on the ladder changed the situation drastically."

Dr. Lindstrom frowned. "You've both been holding back vital information that's preventing any possibility of a true relationship. On her part it's particularly understandable. I'm going to give you a booklet to read that covers many of her feelings. It will help you see into her psyche.

"As for you, a decision has to be made. If you love her and hope to have a permanent relationship with her, then you need to tell her that the next time you're together. No guessing games. Gut honesty is the glue that will lay the groundwork for a lasting relationship. She can't handle anything but the truth."

"You're right. I should have known that."

"How could you have known? This is uncharted territory for both of you. But if knowledge of this assault has changed your mind because you can't deal with the pain, then you must stop seeing her for your sake as well as hers."

"I love her more than ever," Zane said.

"You say that now, but your journey is going to be difficult. She may see herself as a tainted woman, unworthy. Your job will be to help her get past that. It won't be an easy task. If she loves you and admits it, then she'll have to be the one to tell you what she expects now that you know she's been assaulted. You'll have to recognize and accept her feelings as well as your own. You've admitted that your anger is explosive."

Zane nodded.

"Then I don't have to tell you that you must get past that to show her compassion and acceptance. Not every man can do this when it comes to the woman he loves. You'll have to let her make decisions for herself so she can get control over her life. Because of your impatience, you may not like them. Share with her that you will be there when she needs you. My last piece of advice to you is to show your unconditional love and support."

He handed him a booklet and a printout. Zane took them and got to his feet. "I can't thank you enough for seeing me today. I feel better just having talked to you."

"Good. Don't hesitate to call me anytime. While you're here I'll write out another prescription for you."

In a minute Zane left with all the items in hand and headed for the truck. He planned to drive by the dig site and surprise Avery. He'd ask her out for tonight. While he was there, she could introduce him to the crew. The information from the bureau's database search should be in before long and he could put faces with information. Though he didn't believe any of the people on the crew were responsible for the vandalism, he didn't plan to leave a stone unturned.

He stopped to do an errand and ate lunch before leaving Billings. While he waited in the drive-through line, he scanned the printout. It was a list of rules for intimacy with a partner who'd been assaulted. The information was a real eye-opener. He reached for the booklet. One line leaped out at him.

The world is no longer a safe place, so anyone can be a threat and can trigger the fight-or-flight response.

That moment in the trailer came back to haunt him. Zane's first plan was to tell her that he was in love with her, and then he'd take the doctor's last piece of advice. *Show your unconditional love and support.*

Half an hour later he pulled up to the other cars and trucks congregated at the dig site, but there was no sign of Avery. He got out and walked around, letting the crew know he was investigating the case. After asking Dr. Osgood a few questions, he found out she'd taken a personal leave day.

On that disappointing note Zane climbed back in the truck and headed home. When he didn't see her truck at the Bannock ranch, he drove by Sadie and Jarod's house to say hello and play with Ryan. Spending a little time with his nephew was exactly what he needed to unwind before he asked Avery over for a home-cooked meal.

Millie kept food on hand for him. This night had to be perfect for Avery.

DR. MOSER HADN'T BEEN able to meet with Avery until after lunch. During the lengthy session, she broke down in front of the psychologist. When she finally left the office, she got caught in the five o'clock traffic leaving Bozeman. Ten minutes from the ranch her cell phone rang. She checked the caller ID.

Zane. Adrenaline gushed through her veins.

After talking with Dr. Moser, her intention was to carefully distance herself from Zane. He cared for another woman and there was nothing she could do about that. Naturally they'd remain friends, but she would be inaccessible most of the time. It wouldn't cure her heartache, but it would lower her stress level until she moved to the reservation.

Her hand hovered over the phone before she decided to answer. She couldn't just cut him off, but she needed to be cautious.

"Hi, Zane. How was your meeting?"

"Nothing that would make headlines. I'm calling to invite you to dinner tonight. Do you have any plans?"

Just be honest, Avery. "No. I need an early night."

"So do I, but I have to eat and I'd like to pay you back for being willing to help me on the stakeout."

She gripped the phone tighter. "I was a complete failure."

"You're wrong about that. It felt good to have you

with me." The feeling was more than mutual, but she'd ruined it. "I'm not just talking about the inside information you provided on the crew. I've missed our families and that includes you. Please allow me to thank you in the only way I know how. I promise it won't be peanut butter sandwiches. I'm not a bad cook."

Avery was melting fast. One last dinner wouldn't hurt since she'd been the one to offend him without meaning to. "Sadie told me as much."

"Shall we say seven-thirty?"

"That sounds fine. I'll be there. Thank you." Avery clicked off. He had no idea she was on the road. She barely had enough time to make it. While she was still holding the phone, she called her grandfather to tell him she wouldn't be home until nine. There'd be no late night for her.

When she pulled up in front of Zane's house, he was waiting for her on the porch. He looked so good lounging against the post in a black silk shirt and jeans that her legs went weak. The man possessed a sophistication you didn't see in the average cowboy, that was for sure.

Forget his time in the SEALs, he loved ranch life and the mountains with the kind of passion to match hers, otherwise he wouldn't have transplanted himself from San Francisco.

That was what killed her. He'd met another woman. Even though she knew he'd found her attractive, it crushed Avery that she'd never been on his emotional radar.

But because he was such a decent human being and so close with her family, he would always show her def-

erence. She was Jarod's sister after all. Zane had deep
affection for the man who'd married Sadie. Jarod and
Ralph had made it possible for Zane to buy the Corkin ranch. That was why his promise to protect Avery
hadn't been lip service.

"A welcoming committee, too?" she called out to
him with a smile. The best thing to do was maintain
the friendship forged a year ago.

His eyes played over her. They had a glint that told
her he liked what he saw. If he only knew the truth
about her.

Zane straightened at her approach. "I can't get
enough of the blue sky. Have you ever noticed those
cotton balls up there? They're whiter than white. You
can only see that color in nature over Big Sky country."

She looked up into the fading light, knowing what
he meant so exactly it was if he could read her mind.
What he didn't know was that not even the blue of a
Montana sky could match his eyes…

"When Lewis Meriwether came through Montana
in 1805, he said it seemed as if those scenes of visionary enchantment would never end. Then he quoted
one of the Indians, 'I shall vanish and be no more, but
the land and sky over which I now roam shall remain,
and change not.'"

Zane opened the door wider for her. "Maybe now
you'll understand why I enjoy being with you so much.
Every time we're together, you share a portion of your
brilliant mind and enrich me more than you know.
Come in."

"Mmm. I smell rolls baking," Avery said to hide

emotions that were getting the better of her. She followed him through the house and out the doors of the dining room to the patio. A cry of surprise escaped her lips to see the table set with a cloth and cutlery. He'd lit candles around a centerpiece of tulips and daffodils. They had to have come from the garden at the edge of the grass.

She spun around. "I can't believe you've gone to all this trouble."

He cocked his head. "I wanted to. Make yourself comfortable while I bring out the steaks and put them on the grill."

The first thing she noticed was that he didn't try to help her into a chair. Normally he would have. After the way she'd reacted in the trailer, he'd learned his lesson. It pained her that she'd done that to him.

In another few minutes they were eating sour cream topped baked potatoes and sizzling steaks fresh from the grill. He served them a fabulous green salad topped with avocados and a creamy garlic dressing. Millie was probably responsible for the yeast rolls. This was no ordinary dinner. He'd gone to a huge amount of trouble, but she just couldn't figure out why.

"Did you make the chocolate cheesecake from scratch?"

"You like it?"

She finished her coffee. "Have I eaten all of my serving?"

His eyes smiled. "I picked it up on my way out of Billings."

She wiped her mouth with a napkin. "The whole

dinner was delicious. Zane—please don't think I'm being ungrateful, but why have you done this for me? You and I both know there's someone else who might have wanted to be your guest for dinner."

"You mean the woman I mentioned to you?"

"Who else?"

A subtle change came over him. His eyes turned a darker blue and his body stilled. While she waited for an answer, she felt a strange tingling sensation. Then he spoke in that deep voice of his. "What if I told you I'm looking at her?"

Chapter Six

Avery's heart jumped to her throat. Surely she'd misunderstood him. "I—I didn't know you were a tease," she stammered.

"You mean you really had no idea I was talking about you the day of our stakeout?"

She rubbed her temples. "Be serious."

"Avery...the second I met you at Daniel Corkin's funeral, I found myself intensely attracted to you. After staying with you for two weeks, I found myself in love with you. Why else would I have asked you to go on the stakeout with me as soon as I could?"

Blood pounded at every pulse point in Avery's body. Shock waves passed through her, making her go hot, then cold.

"To be honest I'd hoped to transfer back here much sooner. A year is a long time to have to wait for certain dreams to become reality. I was with a few women before I moved from San Francisco, and I've been with a few during my time in Glasgow, but in all honesty you've blown every other woman away. Now that I'm home for good, I want to spend time with you, exclusively."

She stared blindly at the flowers. "I had no idea," she whispered.

"During those two weeks I stayed at your house, I fell hard. You and your brothers are a lot alike, you know that? You're solid and true to yourselves. Those qualities are unique and hard to find in a woman or a man. I admire you more than you know."

Stop talking, Zane. You're killing me. His comments were getting too painful for her. "I don't know what to say."

"I realize this seems to have come out of the blue, but because my former marriage was the result of a whirlwind encounter, I decided not to rush things with you. I've learned the best things in life are worth waiting for. Over their eight years apart, Sadie and Jarod found that out because deep down they knew they could only be happy with each other."

Avery lowered her head. "I'm positive there wasn't a moment in Jarod's life when he didn't know Sadie was the woman for him."

"It happens that way sometimes," he murmured. "It happened that way when I first laid eyes on you. I know I'm eight years older than you, and I have a past. I'm hardly a catch, but I'm hoping you'll give me a chance to get to know you better without my having to find a legitimate excuse of some kind to be with you. This dinner is my way of letting you know how I feel."

Panic set in. *She* was the woman who'd captured his interest?

It was impossible.

Avery's fear was so great, she found herself saying it out loud.

"Why is it impossible?"

She trembled over and over again. "You don't know the real me."

"Not completely, no. That works both ways, hence the point of this dinner. I couldn't do this before now. Too many of my cases kept me away days and weeks at a time. Because of that distance, a relationship with you was always out of the question. When I drove in from Glasgow and saw you with Agent Durant, I was afraid I might have been too late."

She had to clear her throat before she could talk. "You know I won't be seeing him again."

He leaned forward. "But you're being so quiet, I'm starting to wonder if there is someone else in your life."

She eyed him frankly. "No. There's no one." If it was possible to die from a bald-faced lie, she was the prime candidate.

A faint smile broke one corner of his mouth. "I happen to know you're not indifferent to me." She had no doubt her cheeks were glowing hot. "Avery Bannock, would you do me the honor of spending time with me on a daily basis? I've been thinking about it for a whole year and don't want any more wasted time to go by."

While she was still reeling from the one proposal she could never have anticipated coming from him, he shocked her a second time by getting to his feet. "I promised you an early night and I meant it. I'll walk you out. Tomorrow I'll come by the dig site on your lunch hour with a picnic basket and we'll talk."

Her head was spinning.

"Don't worry. If your answer is a flat-out no because I've misread your feelings for me, I'm a big boy and can take the rejection. We'll always be friends and no one will ever know what transpired between us."

Again he allowed her to get up from the table on her own. Zane had a shocking effect on her equilibrium. She started through the house to the porch on shaky legs. He stood aside.

"Zane—"

"We'll talk tomorrow," he interrupted her. "Drive home safely. Text me when you're in the house."

She took a few steps before turning to him. "I will. Thank you for the delicious dinner."

He stayed where he was. "Thank *you* for not shutting me down at the table. At least you've left me with some hope that you were listening."

Hearing those words, she rushed out to the truck and drove away as fast as possible, ignoring his warning. By some miracle she reached the ranch house without incident, but she didn't get out.

What was she going to do? She could hear what her psychologist would say. *The man who assaulted you has been arrested. This man you love has just told you what your heart never expected to hear. Are you brave enough to take the next step? He's left it in your hands.*

Joy and terror warred for supremacy. Avery pressed her forehead to the steering wheel. It took an hour before she finally went inside the house and let him know she was home, but she was still out of answers. The accelerated beat of her heart kept her awake for the rest of the night, knowing she'd see him tomorrow.

ZANE GOT UP at six on Tuesday morning to meet Matt Henson at the pasture. He'd given Zane the job of keeping an eye on the young calves for signs of illness. Matt taught him to look for scours and pneumonia. If they spotted a cow that wouldn't accept its calf or would steal another cow's calf, he would deal with that problem, too.

Around ten-thirty he returned to the house to shower. After making lunch for him and Avery, he checked his email. The news he'd been waiting for from the lab revealed he'd been right about the tracks of an ATV. The foam casts confirmed it had been mounted with Maxxis twenty-five by eight–inch tubeless tires in front, twenty-five by ten–inch tires in the rear.

With some checking he found out that brand and style of tire had only been sold for the past six months. That particular size fit the Honda Rubicon. Two people could fit on it if necessary, but it wasn't advised.

There'd been two sets of footprints inside the grid but they were too faint to be cast. Since no information came back on any of the ATVs registered to members of the archaeological crew, it meant the desecration was probably done by a couple of vandals.

Zane would go to the other vandalized site and see what kind of tracks he could find. If there was a match, he could solve both crimes once he'd apprehended the culprit. The detailed information from the crime lab made it much easier for him to find the dealer where the tires and possibly the ATV were originally purchased and go from there.

He phoned in the information to the police, who would start watching for an ATV of that description. Tonight he'd send out emails to all the known dealerships of all-terrain vehicles in the Billings region where the Honda Rubicon was sold.

A fingerprint had been lifted off one of the Pall Mall Menthol Black cigarette butts. They should have results from the database search on the dig researchers in another twenty-four hours. The peppermint pattie candy wrapper revealed no prints, but could indicate the preference of the culprit if the wind hadn't blown it in from someplace else.

Pleased with this much progress, he returned Margaret's call. After three rings she picked up.

"I'm glad it's you, Zane."

"Sorry it took me this long to get back to you."

"No problem. I thought you might like to hear about the latest gossip. A guy was arrested for stealing artifacts from the Mitchell Indian Village in South Dakota. He did some blabbing.

"There's a network covering Wyoming, South Dakota, Nebraska and Montana. This guy has positively implicated people in the BIA who've been aiding and abetting the transportation of artifacts across state lines. Things are really corrupt, Zane. There's been another theft reported at the Pike-Pawnee Village site in Webster County, Nebraska."

Every time the BIA was mentioned, Zane's thoughts

went to Mike Durant. He didn't like it. He didn't like it at all. "I hear you and I'm indebted to you for this info, Margaret. We'll talk again."

After hanging up, he left for Absarokee. En route he stopped at the only shop in White Lodge selling jet skis, motorcycles and ATVs. After a search, the manager couldn't find a record of a sale of that tire within the past six months. As for the Honda Rubicon, he provided the names and addresses of four owners within the past three years. Zane sent that information to the police after he'd returned to the truck. Now he could cross this business off his list and meet Avery.

Before long he reached the site and found her and a male crew member sifting dirt on a sorting table. They'd set it up in the field near the damaged foundation part of the site. As Zane pulled up next to her truck, their eyes met. She cast him a faint smile before she said something to her partner. The man nodded and kept working while she made her way toward Zane.

It went against his instincts to let her get in the truck by herself, but after reading the material from the booklet the doctor had given him, he knew to be careful. The wrong move could alarm or frighten her. He knew it was essential she remain in control.

"Hi," she said in a quiet voice, closing the passenger door. She pulled off her gloves and turned to put them on the backseat. The sun had brought color to her cheeks. She'd fastened that sensational mane of sable-colored hair at her nape, accentuating the classic oval shape of her face. Today she wore jeans and another snap-up Western shirt, this time in yellow. His dream of being with her all the time was starting to come true. He'd do whatever he could to make it permanent.

"I thought we'd eat at the park over in town." She avoided his eyes during the short drive. He parked the truck beneath some trees facing south toward the Beartooth Mountains. "I hope you're hungry. I brought ham and cheese sandwiches."

"After that wonderful dinner you served last night, you wouldn't think I could be ready for another meal, but I am."

He reached for the basket with their food and the thermos. "Coffee?"

"Not right now, thanks." She took one of the sandwiches and unwrapped the foil.

"Any more signs of damage when you got out here this morning?"

She'd started making inroads on her sandwich. "No, thank heaven. How's the investigation coming?"

"Very well as a matter of fact." He brought her up to speed. "I'm going to catch whoever's doing this."

Her chest rose and fell visibly. "I don't doubt it." She wadded up the foil in her palm.

Zane finished off his cup of coffee and put everything in the backseat. "Since you probably have to rejoin your group at the site before long, I'm anxious to hear what you've decided about us."

In the next breath she turned against the door so she could face him. "There is no us, and never can be."

He'd been ready for that answer. "Because you're not in love with me?"

She averted her eyes, but he could see the nerve

throbbing crazily at the base of her throat. "You're a good family friend, Zane. You know how grateful I am for all you did to help Sadie both in California and here."

That was nice to hear. "Have you forgotten you were the one who put me on to the idea of working for the BLM? You weren't exactly pushing me away with that idea. It was the night of Ralph's birthday party, the night I held you in my arms for the first time while we danced."

Avery couldn't look at him.

"Are you telling me you didn't want to go on dancing with me all night? Or that night in Las Vegas after Liz and Connor left to go back to the trailer? As I recall, neither of us could stand to let go of the other when Jarod signaled that it was time to return to the hotel. How about all those nights at your house when neither of us wanted to go up to bed after your grandfather said good-night?"

A tortured sigh escaped her lips.

He kept on talking. "I couldn't believe that all the time Sadie was dying to be back in Montana with Jarod, he had a sister like you growing up on the Bannock ranch. I thought I must be hallucinating that the most beautiful woman I'd ever met seemed to want my company. Though we didn't act on our feelings, we ached for each other, Avery. We're aching for each other now. Those aren't the feelings of a person who only wants to be a friend. We're beyond that."

"Even if I don't deny that," she said, "what you're suggesting won't work for us."

Dr. Lindstrom's warning rang in his ears. *Your journey is going to be difficult. She may see herself as a tainted woman, unworthy. Your job will be to help her get past that. It won't be an easy task.*

"Why don't you think on it a little more? I'll come by for you after you get home from work this evening. I thought we'd take a ride in the mountains. It's possible we'll see some wild horses. There's supposed to be a bright moon. We won't need the goggles tonight."

"Are you inviting my brothers, too?"

She hadn't forgotten what he'd said about them going in a group. Since she hadn't said no, he made a snap decision.

"I'll get home before you and call them. Give me a ring after you're back at the ranch and we'll go from there. But before we do anything else, we need to exchange cell phone numbers."

Tight bands constricted his lungs until she pulled the phone out of her purse. Filled with elation that she was going along with him to this extent, he reached for his phone and programmed in the numbers. "I've kept you long enough and had better let you get back to work."

She remained quiet on the mile drive to the site. He half expected her to beg off their plans, but when they arrived, all she did was thank him for the sandwiches and climb out of the cab. After she'd joined the others, he left for the Bannock ranch to find Jarod.

After making a phone call, he discovered him mending fences on the eastern side of the property. The moment Jarod saw the truck headed toward him, he stopped what he was doing and walked up to Zane who jumped down from the cab.

The two men studied each other for a quiet moment. "I've just come from having lunch with Avery. You need to know about something that happened the other night while we were at the dig site in the trailer."

His black eyes narrowed. "Go ahead."

"Our first hunch about her was correct."

The grim look on Jarod's face took on a savage cast. "She told you she was assaulted?"

"No, but the proof was there." He spent the next few minutes telling him about her self-defense move and the hidden pistol. "I talked to my psychologist in Billings yesterday morning. He agreed that she's likely suffering from PTSD and gave me a booklet to help me understand how to help her."

Zane reached in his back pocket and handed it to Jarod. "I've already read it. You and Connor need to read it, too. One more thing. I took the doctor's advice. Last night I invited her for a special dinner. Later I told her I'd fallen in love with her and wanted to start seeing her on an exclusive basis."

Jarod took a swift breath. "How did that go over?"

"Obviously she was shaken and said a lot of things to put me off, but she didn't give me a flat-out no. Considering my situation, a quarter of a loaf is better than none."

"When it comes to Avery, I agree."

"I've asked her to go for a horseback ride in the mountains when she gets home from work this evening. We'll look for some wild horses. I made the suggestion that maybe you and Connor could come with us. She grabbed on to the idea. Before I can move forward with her, she has to learn to trust me."

"If Sadie weren't so close to her delivery date…"

"I thought about that, but maybe Connor and Liz will come with us."

Jarod tipped his cowboy hat back. "Tell you what. I'll phone him and tell him everything you told me."

"Good, but this information stays with the three of us."

"No one else can ever know," came Jarod's fierce response.

"Then we understand each other."

"When I get home, I'll phone him to find out if he and Liz would like to go riding with you. After my talk with him, I'm sure they'll join you no matter what other plans they might have had."

"I owe you, Jarod."

"You've got that the wrong way around. I didn't tell you everything Uncle Charlo told me when I confided in him about Avery. He said that through the Great Spirit, her imprisoned spirit would be freed by one with great vision who would have to follow it as the eagle seeks the deepest blue of the sky."

Jarod's black eyes bore holes into him. "I didn't understand the full significance of his words until Sadie told me something her mother confided to her about you and your brother. Your parents gave him the Greek name *Timothy* which means 'honoring God.' They gave *you* the Hebrew name *Zane* which means, '*from* God.'"

Gooseflesh broke out over Zane's body.

FOUR ON HORSEBACK made it to the top of a cliff above the Crooked Creek Road. With the help of a full moon, they were able to see a sweep of gullies, part of the Hitting Rock Mountains, so named by the Crow Nation for the flint they found here.

Avery's heart pounded in anticipation while they waited to see if the wild mustangs were running through this area tonight. Zane sidled his gelding next to her mare while Connor and Liz rode on a little farther.

"Do me a favor and say the Crow name for the Pryor Mountains again, Avery. I need to learn it."

"Baahpuuo Isawaxaawuua."

He tried repeating it back, but had trouble with the pronunciation. They both chuckled. "I'll keep practicing. Now tell me why these are called the Pryors."

"Sergeant Nathaniel Hale Pryor was a member of the Lewis and Clark Expedition. He tried to catch horses stolen from the expedition in this area and the name stuck. During that period he recorded lithic scatters that contained hearths and lost stone tools. He also made note of both vertebrate and invertebrate fossils. That's why the Crooked Creek Natural Landmark is a National Register site."

He smiled in the moonlight. "With you as my human encyclopedia, I'm the luckiest agent in the field."

"Except that tonight I don't know if we'll see any horses." She was still so stunned by his admission that he'd fallen in love with her, her life seemed surreal at the moment and she felt at a loss for words. A light breeze blew her hair around. "You need luck to find them. The problem is, like all ferals they generally avoid human contact and are easily spooked."

"Except for Firebrand," he reminded her.

"Connor broke that horse through a lot of time and patience."

She felt his gaze on her.

"Firebrand's a real champion."

"The best!" she exclaimed. "One of the reasons why is because the Spanish ferals have a natural paso gait. They're sure-footed and possess a lot of stamina. If they bond with a human, it's for life. Both he and Jarod have had great success with the ferals. I know Connor's feral stud farm is going to take off."

"I have no doubt that it will. How did the ferals get here?"

"Long Hair maintains that they were brought here about 1725. The explorers discovered large numbers of them in the 1740s. But to answer your question, historians say they are direct descendants of the Barb horses brought to North America in the early 1600s. The Spaniard conquistador Juan de Oñate brought an expedition to explore America north of the Rio Grande. Their history is fascinating."

"How big was it?"

"He led several expeditions, but the largest one he undertook went east to the Great Plains. It was huge—one hundred and thirty Spanish soldiers, priests, servants and three hundred and fifty horses and mules. He founded settlements, hence the origin of the horses. Their bloodline runs through Firebrand and Jarod's horse Chief. Kind of exciting to think about, but they don't seem to be around tonight and it's getting late."

"I can handle it." His eyes still rested on her. "It's incredibly mystical up here and there'll be many other nights in the years to come. We've got all the time in the world."

He kept saying *we*. How could there be a *we*? Once he knew about her, she feared what she'd see in those hot blue eyes. For now they were watching her with a look that melted her bones. But once he knew the truth, that look would be replaced by one of repulsion he wouldn't be able to hide no matter how hard he tried.

She took a deep breath. "It's getting late. Let's find the others and head back. We all have work tomorrow."

After studying her for a minute longer, Zane called to them that they were leaving.

"We're right behind you," Connor shouted back from a distance.

As they made their way down, Avery thought about all the years she'd ridden up here with her brothers, or with Cassie and the girls. This was the first time in her life she'd come up here with a man.

There went that ping in her heart again just thinking about Zane. She loved him more than he would ever know. He was the only man she'd ever felt this way about. Wearing a cowboy hat, he looked fantastic mounted on his horse and rode like a pro. Put him next to Jarod and Connor and you'd never know which one of them was the new cowboy.

Another rush of warmth passed through her. *He wants to be with me.*

Avery couldn't take it in. Tears spilled down her cheeks because she knew this euphoria couldn't possibly last. She needed to enjoy it now. Zane had made his intentions clear and expected to hear something definitive back, but he was giving her time to think everything through.

But even he would run out of patience before long and needed to hear the words that either meant planning a future with her or not. She wiped the tears from her eyes, hating how emotional she'd become around him.

When they reached the dirt road he slowed down and looked over his shoulder at her. Hopefully he couldn't see what a mess she'd turned into when he wasn't looking. "Race you back to the ranch."

"You're on!" She galloped past him. "Come on, Snowball. Let's show Zane what we're made of."

She could hear the thunder of hooves behind her and increased her speed. The joy of being with Zane had filled her with an excess of energy. She never wanted this fun to end. They flew across Bannock property toward the barn. She beat him to Snowball's stall, but deep down she knew he'd held back so she could be the winner. Avery dismounted in a burst of laughter.

He rode up to her with that killer smile of his, guaranteed to turn her heart over. Looking down at her he said, "Damn, if you aren't a speed demon. I doubt I'll ever be able to best you. You left the others in the dust."

"Damn, if you aren't a terrific liar," she fired back with a grin as she removed her horse's saddle and bridle. "Striker's not even breathing hard." After putting everything in the tack room, she made certain there was water and hay before she walked out of the barn.

Zane followed alongside her, still astride his horse. "I'll accompany you to the house, then I'll head home."

They made their way over to the ranch house in a landscape bathed by the moon. "Can you take off early tomorrow? Say two o'clock? I'd like you to come to a new site where some hikers have reported vandalism. I need your expert eye to help evaluate how much damage was done."

Needing to be with him again was like needing air to breathe. She spoke without hesitation. "I'll leave for work early so it won't be a problem."

"Since I'll be up at dawn, I'll drive you to Absarokee so you can leave your truck at home. When I come by the site to pick you up later in the day, I'll be happy to tell Dr. Osgood it's for official business."

"That won't be necessary. He'll understand. We all want you to catch these criminals." She paused at the front door. "Tomorrow I'll buy dinner for us."

"I can't wait." He tipped his black cowboy hat at her. "Expect me at six-thirty in the morning."

"I'll be ready." She slipped inside the house and raced up to her room where she collapsed on the bed.

Zane... The more wonderful he was, the more terrified she was growing. A sense of doom enveloped her. He'd revealed his feelings for her and told her about his divorce and his PTSD up front. To keep her secret from him now was the worst thing she could do.

Tomorrow night on the way home, she'd tell him the truth. She didn't have a choice, not when he'd opened his heart to her. It would be the end of any relationship they might have had. But as Dr. Moser had said, there could be no foundation without honesty.

Tragically, there would be no foundation once he knew the truth, winding up in a no-win situation. She'd known her destiny on the night she'd been assaulted. That was when her life had changed forever.

Chapter Seven

Zane walked out to the truck with his gear Wednesday morning under an overcast sky. According to the forecast, they'd have some rain showers over the next few days. But nothing could dampen his spirits as he drove over to the Bannock ranch to pick up Avery.

He phoned to let her know he was coming. As always, the sight of her set off sparks. She came down the porch steps dressed in jeans and a soft suede tan vest with fringe that hung loose over a light blue T-shirt. He reached across the seat to open the door for her.

Today she'd done her hair in a braid. Though he loved it loose, the pulled-back style showed off her gorgeous face. Their gazes met. "Hi," she said, sounding the slightest bit out of breath as she climbed into the cab. Her tiny glass earrings shaped like buttercups gave off glints of blue and green with a center of gray that matched her incredible eyes.

"Where did you get those earrings?"

"On the reservation. They're made of dichroic glass."

"Explain *dichroic*."

"The artisan works with a composite of nontranslucent glass. When stacking layers with microlayers of oxides and metals, it causes the glass to shift colors."

"Nice," he whispered.

"They *are* unusual."

Just like Avery herself. He backed around and they headed for Absarokee. "How's Ralph?"

"Wonderful. I can't believe he's the same person from a year ago. This morning he ate a big breakfast and is going to drive up to the pasture with Jarod later on. The doctor has warned him not to overdo it, but I guess if he's feeling good enough to get out like that, then he should."

Zane nodded. "Your grandfather's work ethic would make it impossible for him to sit around if he's feeling well enough to leave the house."

"You're right. He was always a human dynamo."

"Both of my grandfathers died when I was young, so I hardly remember them. Yours has been spared to bring you and your brothers a lot of happiness."

"After my parents were killed in that lightning storm, I don't know what my life would have been like without my grandparents."

Yet not even her grandparents had been able to shield her from one of the worst atrocities a human could face. He had to suppress the sudden feeling of rage against the man who'd attacked her, robbing her in a way that had erased her trust in life, her joy… Zane doubted he'd ever be able to let go of his anger.

She turned her head toward him. "How's the case progressing?"

"So far, no background evidence on your crew has come back to raise any flags, but I'm beginning to get responses to my emails. This morning there were four messages from various ATV dealers. They've all sent proof of sales with names and addresses for Maxxis tires purchased within the past five months. Three of the dealers are here in Billings. The one from Laurel, fifteen miles away from here, reported the sale of a new Honda Rubicon.

"I'll visit all the addresses they sent and do a little investigating while you work. Then I'll come by the dig site and we'll drive up to the mountains not far from where we were last night to take a look at the vandalized site."

Their drive was over way too soon for Zane, who wanted to lean toward her and kiss her thoroughly, which was out of the question. She jumped down from the truck and waved him off before joining the others.

Once in Billings he used his GPS to locate the addresses of customers who'd bought that particular size and brand of tire recently. In two of the cases, the owners were grandparents who were getting their equipment ready for children and grandchildren descending for the summer. They didn't mind him inspecting their ATVs. As for cigarettes, neither couple had ever smoked. He bagged dirt from the treads of both vehicles and left.

The other owner was a single man in his thirties. Zane went to see him in his office at a paper-supply company, first introducing himself to the manager to let him know he was on official business. He found out the guy didn't smoke as far as his employer knew. The owner of that ATV said he used it for pleasure rides with his friends.

If Zane wanted to see it, he could follow him home and he'd unlock the garage where he kept it. Zane went to the man's apartment and inspected his vehicle, bagging the dirt from inside the tread. He thanked him and left for Laurel.

The sky had grown darker. He smelled rain in the air as he pulled up to the ranch house on the outskirts of the town. According to the store manager in Laurel, the guy who bought the new Honda Rubicon was a well-to-do local cattle rancher named Lester Newell. The guy from the dealership was really talkative. When he found out Zane was a rancher, he became a font of information. Zane learned he'd done business with the Newells off and on for years. He knew the family pretty well.

Two of their grown children were married. Lester's other two sons were single and in their twenties. The one named Terry worked out on the ranch with his dad. The other one, Steve, was away at college in Missoula.

Zane drove up to the ranch house, wanting to talk to Mr. Newell. No one answered. He walked around the back to get a good look at everything. As far as he could see, this rancher owned several trucks, a four-wheel drive, a car, an inboard-outboard boat, a fishing boat, kayaks, Jet Skis, a horse trailer, a motor home, an ATV with a trailer for it—every toy you could think of.

On the way back to his truck, one of the ranch hands

called to him from his tractor. Zane said, "I'm here to see Mr. Newell on ranch business."

"You're out of luck. He's gone to a funeral in Helena, but he'll be back tomorrow. You can talk to his foreman."

"No, thanks. I'll try to reach Mr. Newell later." Zane didn't leave his name and took off. He'd come back after dark and do a little evidence gathering. Pleased with today's progress, he left town and headed for the dig site eager to pick up Avery.

"Sorry I'm late," he called from the window as he drove up to her.

She shook her head after getting in the truck. "Ten minutes is nothing."

They headed out. "I think I've stumbled on to some real evidence." He spent the rest of the time telling her what he'd discovered.

Avery shivered. "You're so good at this, it's scary."

"What these thieves and vandals do is scary."

"I know. Artifacts are disappearing at an alarming rate."

He drove them up the mountain road under a threatening sky. Avery guided him to one of several sacred Crow spots along the way so he could see what they looked like. When he stopped the truck, she got out and ran over to the edge of the cliff. He heard her cry out.

Zane hurried over to where she stood. "What's wrong?"

She turned a white face to him. "The main structure is gone!"

"What do you mean 'main structure'?"

He could see there'd been an explosion of some kind, like a great scab against the landscape. Some rubble and broken rocks were all that remained. Grabbing gloves and an evidence bag, he scooped up some soil and debris to put in the truck. In the morning he'd express mail it to the crime lab.

Avery stood at the edge of the cliff. "Everything was blown all over!" she cried with tears running down her pale cheeks. "This was a sacred place where a person could lie down on his fasting bed. Jarod came to one of these places. Maybe even this one."

Her moan shook him to the foundations.

"Picture a coffin shape with walls of wood and rock about four feet long and two feet high. The structure had a nest-like feature with the long-axis oriented east to west so the person could face the morning star while they waited for their dream. That was the time they felt closest to the spirit. Oh, Zane—"

She wept so bitterly, he forgot everything but the need to comfort her. In the next instant he wrapped his arms around her and rocked her for a long time. Avery sobbed into his neck as rain began to pelt them.

"How can there be such evil in the world?" She pounded her fists into his upper arms and shoulders covered by his sweatshirt. "This was their sacred place."

He had no words. The only comfort he could offer was his body. Her outpouring of grief came from her soul where she suffered agony beyond what she'd found here. He was thankful she could let some of it out and not try to push him away because of their closeness.

"Come on," he finally murmured against her forehead. "Let's get back in the truck before we're soaked to the skin." At this high elevation the temperature had dropped.

Half carrying her, they made it to the cab. He turned on the engine and started up the heater so she wouldn't chill. He always carried emergency supplies in the backseat and threw a blanket over her.

"Here." The rain pounded down as he handed her the thermos. "The coffee will warm you." Her PTSD could send her into shock if he didn't take care of her. The evidence of desecration was so horrendous to comprehend, he feared she might not get over it. Zane knew he wouldn't.

Someone had a vendetta, reminding him of Ned, whose bigotry had almost cost Jarod his life. But to come up to the mountains and blow up sacred ground was the act of someone who was out of his or her mind.

"I'm taking you home now." He reached in back for the sack that held a peanut butter sandwich he hadn't eaten yet. She needed food. "Here. Eat this." Zane put it in her hands. "I'll hurry."

By the time they'd left the mountain, the rain had stopped. He drove directly to her ranch, but when he started to turn onto the road leading to her ranch house, she spoke up. "Do you mind if we go to your house first? I need to talk to you and don't want to disturb my grandfather."

Nothing could have made him happier. "Are you sure?"

"That's my question for you. I know you're hungry.

Since I promised you dinner on me, how about I make *you* an omelet. After the way you helped me earlier tonight, I owe you."

Once they entered his house and had freshened up, they made dinner together. When he suggested she remove her suede vest to let it dry, she said she was fine and for him not to worry about it. Zane let it go. Now that the shock was wearing off, he didn't want to do anything that would make her run. She'd let him hold her tonight without flinching. A far cry from what had happened in the trailer.

They sat at the table to eat. "I'm going to capture those criminals, Avery."

"I know you will, but that isn't what I want to talk to you about."

"If it concerns what you did to me with your elbow while we were in the trailer, I'm way ahead of you." He couldn't hold back any longer.

She didn't flinch. "I want to explain about that," she said.

"You don't have to." He took a deep breath. "Avery," he began, "I felt your weapon before I backed away. To be honest, I'm thankful that after you were assaulted, you took steps to make sure it never happened again."

She pushed herself away from the table and stood up white-faced. He could tell she was trembling. "How do you know I was assaulted?"

"Your PTSD gave you away long before the other night in the trailer. Your brothers believe it happened either right before you went away to college in Bozeman, or right after you got there."

"Jarod and Connor know?" she said, her voice anguished.

"Let's say they've speculated about it in private for years, but I was the one who brought it up to Jarod a few days ago. All three of us have feared it might have been Ned."

"It wasn't," she said so fast he believed her.

Her brothers would be relieved on that score, but the crime was still there, having been committed by someone else. Avery's terror took her beyond tears. "Who else knows?"

"No one, and no one else ever will. If you'll let me, I want to help you through this."

Her hands formed fists. "No you don't. I couldn't bear your revulsion or your pity."

He folded his arms. "What if I'd been the one assaulted? Would you pity me?"

"Don't play games with me, Zane. This is far too serious."

"I couldn't agree more. A man or a woman can be assaulted by a man or a woman. If I told you it had happened to me, what would be your response?"

She stared at him in horror. "I don't believe it happened to you, and it's not the same thing."

"It's exactly the same thing when you find yourself violated and stripped of your ability to fight back." He walked around the table toward her. "Did you go to the police when it happened?"

AVERY COULDN'T BELIEVE her secret was out. Zane had seen through her from the first time they'd met.

"Yes. Just this past Monday the detective who's been working on my case for eight years informed me that the police have arrested the man who assaulted me and two other victims."

Zane swallowed hard. "That's a huge blessing."

She bowed her head. "I know what you're going to ask next. The answer is yes, I've been seeing a therapist in Bozeman from the first week it happened. I don't know what I would have done without her help."

Gratified by that answer, there was another question he had to ask. The hardest one. "Did you use that self-defense maneuver against me because you're afraid of me?"

Avery threw her head back. "No. You've never given me any reason to distrust you. But I was afraid that if you discovered I was wearing a pistol, you'd demand to know the reason why."

"Which means you didn't want to have to explain the horror of your experience to another person."

"Yes, absolutely. Besides the doctor at the hospital in Bozeman, only the police and Dr. Moser know what happened to me. Now I have to add you to that list. It's one too many."

"I'm not just anyone, Avery. I love you."

A caustic laugh escaped her lips. "You can't."

"I've had my heart set on you for a year. Ask me why I sought you out the second I got home from Glasgow. Suspecting what I did about the trauma behind your PTSD made no difference to me. Now that I know the truth, I love you more for your courage. Despite your pain and fears, you've gone on with your life and you've excelled in so many ways, I can't begin to count them."

"But you don't see me the way a normal man sees a normal woman."

"Who's normal? Define it for me. I know I'm not. When I met you at the funeral, I didn't see a mark on your forehead that meant you were untouchable. What I saw was this exciting woman Sadie had talked about long before we came to Montana. I saw you look at me, too. You know the kind of look I mean. In that moment I felt something that had never happened to me before, not even with my first wife."

"Zane—"

"Let me finish. I could have flown back to San Francisco after the funeral was over, but I didn't because something inside me told me my future was here. But Ralph Bannock's granddaughter lived next door and deserved a hell of a lot more than what I had to give her at the time, so I got busy in order to be worthy of her."

She put up her hands. "Don't say any more, Zane."

"Why not? What is it you don't want to hear?"

"You've got this all turned around. For lack of better words, I'm soiled goods."

"I realize that's the way you feel because of the assault. I can't change your perception of yourself, but this far-from-normal man who has PTSD and dozens of other faults you don't know about yet wants to marry you, anyway."

Avery gasped. *"Marry—"*

"Of course. I want to live with you forever with Ralph's blessing. If you can't say yes to me yet, I'll wait as long as it takes because I'm not going anywhere else and don't want anyone else. Jacob had to wait seven years for Rachel. If he could do it, so can I."

She bit her lip. "You don't mean it."

"Try me," he fired back. "To be honest, I'd like to get married within the next month so we can just be together without always having to make up excuses. The physical side of our marriage can come later when you're ready. I'm not asking for that. If there are problems, we'll deal with them. What's important to me is that we're together all the time under one roof. I want to protect you and I can't be apart from you any longer."

Zane was telling her wonderful things she hadn't even imagined in her dreams.

"This past year has been a nightmare. Admit that it killed you, too, when we had to say goodbye at the airport in Las Vegas. I came close to tossing it all in and begging you to marry me at the first wedding chapel I could find. I had this plan for us to live in Glasgow, and I didn't care that you would have to leave your work for a while. That's how badly I wanted you with me."

He had no idea she'd wanted the same thing.

"Shame on me for not acting on my instincts, but my fear of not being able to provide for you the way I wanted to held me back from saying anything. I wanted to come home to the ranch able to support you and offer you the fabulous life I know we can make together. The rest will come because I refuse to let the dark side of life defeat us. All you have to do is tell me that you love me."

She hugged her arms to her waist. "I think you're

the most amazing man I've ever known, but I can't say those words yet, Zane."

"I can be patient."

His confidence was one of his most appealing qualities. More than ever she didn't feel she deserved him. "Maybe I won't ever be able to say them, but I'm touched to the core that you've said them to me."

His gaze swept over her. "You're shivering. Let's get you home before you catch a chill. Being out in the rain soaked your vest." Zane was aware of everything and took perfect care of her.

He reached for his keys and they left the house in his truck. Before long he pulled up in front of the ranch house. "Tomorrow I'm planning to run in to White Lodge to do some shopping for Ryan. When will you be off work?"

"I leave the dig site at four-thirty."

"How about we meet at Fairchild's around five? You can help me pick out some clothes and toys for my nephew. I need a woman's advice. Then we can go for dinner at El Farol."

His marriage proposal had changed everything. The incredible things he'd confessed to her had illuminated her world. This fabulous man wanted her for his wife. Was it really possible?

Avery knew how she felt about him. And how could she turn down an invitation that included doing something fun for the cutest little boy in the world? Good looks and charm ran in the Lawson family from the oldest to the youngest.

"I'll try to be there on time."

"I'll wait out in front. Get a good sleep, Avery."

She longed to throw herself into his arms. If she agreed to marry him, she could be in his arms every night of her life. Heat engulfed her before she hurried into the house and up the stairs. But by the time she got ready for bed, she was in a new state of agony. What he'd said about putting the physical aspect of their marriage aside until she was ready revealed his deep sensitivity. But what if they did start to make love and then she had a flashback or felt sick?

How many rejections would have to happen before he could no longer handle it? To hurt him like that would add a new dimension to her level of guilty pain. He was doing everything in the world to reassure her, but the time would come when he'd lose patience. No man could be put off indefinitely without regretting his decision to marry.

After removing her clothing, she put her pistol on the dresser and stepped into the shower. Her thoughts flew back to the incident in the trailer. When she'd reacted to his touch, he'd accepted it without a postmortem because he was a master at what he did for a living.

To her shock he'd recognized her PTSD a year ago. While they were in the trailer, he'd discovered she wore a weapon. It was as if he had X-ray vision. She would never be able to hide anything from him.

At first she was outraged that Zane had discussed her behavior with her brothers. But that was in the heat of the moment. Having calmed down, she found she was actually relieved he'd been the one to talk to them. Now that she'd admitted that she'd been assaulted, Zane would communicate that information to them so she wouldn't have to say anything.

Even suspecting what had happened to her, they loved her. She'd always felt their love. Her love for them was greater than ever because they'd never invaded her space, never pressured her or made her uncomfortable.

Zane on the other hand had forced the issue into the open with that forthright manner of his. His excuse that he wanted to marry her was still too incredible for her to comprehend. He hadn't even kissed her yet. Yet how many times had she wanted to feel his mouth on hers while they'd been dancing. He'd been right about them aching for each other.

Oh, Zane. Avery wanted to marry him, but it could end up in disaster.

AT ONE IN the morning, Zane drove back to Laurel, armed with a search warrant. He parked at the side of the road leading into the Newell ranch and went the rest of the way on foot carrying a backpack that held his paraphernalia.

The place was quiet. If there was a dog, it hadn't started barking. Zane crouched down and tried to open the door of the Buick, but it was locked. He had better luck with the Sentra. The ashtray held half a dozen cigarette butts. Zane bagged several. In the process he saw a number of tools on the floor under the glove compartment including a pair of EOD cord/fuse cutters normally used by the military.

Well, well, well.

What could the son be doing with an expensive pair

of cutters like those? If any dynamiting was going on at the ranch, why were the cutters in the Sentra? He took dirt samples from the tire treads as well as from the ATV's tires and bagged the evidence.

Might as well check the entire property in case explosives had been hidden. The federal forest facility that had stored dynamite was only ten miles away. Explosives had been used to blow up those signs at the Shepherd Ah Nei Recreation area. But it would have taken more than one person to pull it off.

He eyed the big trailer parked at the rear of the ranch house. It was the size of Connor's and would be a perfect spot to store five hundred pounds of explosives. One of those trucks could have pulled that trailer, and another truck the ATV trailer. If necessary Zane would be back later to bag traces of dirt from their treads and check the odometers.

Relieved he hadn't been seen, Zane hurried back to his truck. On the way to the highway he notified the twenty-four-hour dispatch at the BLM in Helena to check out the other son. Zane intended to learn his whereabouts the night the dig site in Absarokee, as well as the Ah Nei Recreation area, had been vandalized. He reminded them to check the car's odometer and get evidence from the tread.

Could this be a father and sons' operation? Or the plan of two brothers? Or even one brother and a friend? Any or all theories were possible.

By Thursday evening the clouds were dispersing. No more rain. The air was fresh and clean as Zane and Avery walked out of the store loaded with gifts.

"Ryan will love his new Big Wheel."

"I agree. He can tear around my house all he wants. You'll have to come home with me so we can put it and the red wagon together."

Her smile thrilled him. "He loves to haul things around."

They'd picked out a blow-up swimming pool to put in the backyard. She'd chosen a SpongeBob SquarePants bathing suit along with some shorts and tops. Zane put everything in the back of the truck, then drove them to the Mexican restaurant a couple of blocks over from the store. After locking the truck, they went inside. He asked the manager to seat them in the back where they could have some privacy.

Since he'd left Dr. Lindstrom's office on Monday, Zane had been formulating a plan and hoped it wouldn't backfire on him tonight. While they ate dinner he told her how his cases were progressing. As soon as he had word from the crime lab about the findings of the other brother's car, he'd make arrests.

For dessert he ordered sopaipillas. When Avery was halfway through hers, Zane pulled a little unwrapped box from his jeans' pocket and put it next to her water glass.

Her soft gray eyes widened. "What's this?"

"You helped me with my shopping and deserve a gift, too."

"I didn't see you buy anything for me."

His mouth broke into a faint smile. "You wouldn't have. I picked it up when I was in Las Vegas, but the time wasn't right to give it to you."

The words *Las Vegas* charged the atmosphere around

them. She stared at the box as if she were afraid of it. He watched that nerve throbbing in the base of her throat, the one he wanted to kiss away.

"I promise you it won't bite if you open it."

A nervous laugh escaped her lips.

"As I told you the other night, I was ready to marry you while we were there for Connor and Liz."

Her hand trembled as she laid her fork on the plate. She was unable to look at him.

"Since you seem to need help, I'll do the honors." He took off the lid and pulled out the ring box. Using both hands, he opened it to reveal a one-carat solitaire diamond set in gold nestled against black velvet. In the light from the small lantern on their table, the stone dazzled the eye.

"I'm asking you to marry me, Avery. This makes it official. I told you I'm a patient man. You don't need to answer yes or no right now, but you need to understand the full extent of my commitment to you. I've loved you for a long time." He put the box down, leaving it open to her gaze. "If you can't wear it yet, keep it until you know your own heart."

The wounded sound she made caught him on the raw. "I was a virgin until I was violated by another man. I'll never be the same person again."

He took a swift breath. "That was the act of a predator who committed a horrific crime. The real you in your heart and soul remains untouched, waiting for love. I consider myself the luckiest man in the world to be sitting here across from you, hoping you'll accept this ring."

Her glistening hair flowed around her shoulders. He felt the beauty of her soul and it electrified him. "I don't know if I can ever give myself to you, Zane."

"Just answer one question. Do you love me?"

Slowly she raised her head and stared into his eyes. "Yes. I've loved you from the beginning."

Those words made him euphoric. "Do you believe that true love conquers all?"

"I thought I did until this happened to me. Now I don't know," she said in a tremulous voice.

"Then let's get married and find out."

Her hand went to her throat. "What if I can't love you the way you want and deserve to be loved by your wife?"

"What if you *can*?" he fired back. "In the meantime we'll hold each other when you want to be held. When I'm your husband, I swear I'll never do anything you don't want me to."

"That's no marriage for you."

"I couldn't marry another woman feeling like I do about you."

"That could change with time."

"So could your feelings for me. We have to have faith that our marriage can work. If you want to say vows in a civil ceremony at the courthouse with no one else, we can do that."

"No—" she asserted with enough force that he knew she meant it. "I couldn't do that to my family. It's all or nothing."

Thank the Lord.

"Do me a favor and wear it home. Sleep with it

tonight and think about everything. I'll come by the house tomorrow after we're both home from work. If you're not wearing it, then I'll know you need more time." He leaned forward. "Will you let me put it on you?"

"I'm afraid, Zane."

"So am I." *Always let her be in control.* "To be honest, I'm terrified you won't lift your left hand for me to do the honors."

A minute must have gone by before he saw movement and she shyly extended it. Before she could change her mind he clasped her hand with a gentle touch and slid the diamond home on her ring finger.

She studied it in the light. The shimmer of the diamond matched the shimmer in her wet eyes. "It's breathtaking."

"On you it is. I've dreamed of doing this for months. I love you, Avery."

After lowering her eyes she said, "Do you mind if we leave now?"

"I was just going to suggest it." They still had the rest of the night ahead of them.

While she reached for the box and put everything in her purse, he left a tip. Together they got up and walked through the crowded restaurant to the cashier. Once he'd paid for dinner, they got in the truck. "I'll drive you to your truck and follow you home."

A few minutes later as he was pulling into the parking space next to her truck, her phone rang. She checked the caller ID. "It's my grandfather. I wonder why he's calling." After she'd clicked on and said hello to him, Zane didn't have to wait long for the answer. "I'll go there right now, Grandpa, then call you back."

The second she hung up, she turned to Zane with nervous excitement. "Sadie went into labor in the middle of the night and is still in labor. Jarod took her to the hospital at eleven this morning. She wasn't due quite yet. They're trying to slow down the contractions, but it might not be working."

"Sounds like Little Sits in the Center is tired of sitting and wants to make his presence known."

"Zane." She half laughed.

"Let's drive over and see what's going on. We can come by for your truck later on." He backed out and they headed for the hospital at the other end of town.

"Knowing my brother, he's having a heart attack about now. He's brave for everything and everyone except when it comes to Sadie. When she got that terrible morning sickness in the beginning, he fell apart. I can only imagine what he's like now."

He smiled at her. "Eileen had bad morning sickness with Ryan. Like mother, like daughter. But they're nearing the end now." Zane was envious of Jarod, who had a wife he adored and a baby on the way.

Someday soon, Avery.

Chapter Eight

After Zane drove them to the hospital, they hurried up to the second floor maternity lounge where they met Connor and Liz. Matt and Millie were with them. Avery rushed forward. "What's the latest news? Grandpa said they were trying to slow down her contractions."

"It didn't work. That baby is coming now."

No sooner had they all hugged than Jarod's uncle Charlo, the tribal elder everyone revered, arrived with his wife, Pauline. Avery left Zane's side to give them hugs. "Did Grandpa call you, too?"

Pauline nodded. "He did, but two hours before that my husband said we had to go to the hospital because Sits in the Center needed us."

The moment she spoke those amazing words, a gaunt Jarod came into the lounge looking like death. His dark, anxiety-filled eyes took all of them in. "There's a problem. Sadie's been in labor too long. She's exhausted so they're going to do a cesarean section."

"That's good," Liz said, trying to reassure him. "They'll get the baby out quickly."

The family waited, distracting themselves with quiet conversations or, in some cases, closing their eyes for a rest. Avery watched as Charlo approached his nephew with those wise, farseeing eyes. "No need to fear. Your mother is close. In the night I heard your son singing praises during his four-day fast."

With those prophetic words spoken like the patriarch he was, the hairs prickled on the back of Avery's neck. She and Connor exchanged a silent glance of wonder before Jarod nodded to his uncle and disappeared.

Avery's gray eyes swerved to Zane. "Did you hear that?" she whispered.

"We all heard it right down to our bones. Not every father-to-be has a visionary uncle like Charlo."

"It *has* to be a good sign, Zane. You saw the shape Jarod is in."

"I see a woman who loves her big brother very much."

"Probably too much," she admitted.

His brows lifted. "Is there such a thing as too much? I felt the same way about Tim."

She searched his eyes. "I'm sorry you and Ryan lost him."

"Me, too, but out of that loss my nephew gained a new father in Jarod, a man who has become my good friend. Even better, he has a sister I love."

They all waited another half hour. Then Connor came in the lounge. "Come on, everyone. The nurse says we can go to Sadie's room now."

Zane and Avery followed behind the others. They walked down the hall and through the doors to the birthing room. When she saw Jarod sitting next to a tired-looking Sadie while she held their baby, her throat swelled with emotion. Both exhausted parents glowed.

Between the family and staff, joyous pandemonium broke out. Avery reached out to hang on to Zane's arm without thinking. Leaning close to him she whispered, "I thought we'd see a cap of black hair, but he has a trace of blond hair like Sadie's and looks perfect."

He hugged her arm tighter. "I'm sure Jarod's in there somewhere."

She looked up at him. "My brother's fighting tears. I've never seen him do that before. He loves her so much I think he's suffered more than she has through the whole pregnancy."

"Jarod lost his mother before he could know her. It's no wonder."

Millie held the baby for a minute. "Have you thought of a name yet, honey?"

Sadie turned to her husband. "We've decided on Colin Matthew Ralph Charlo Bannock."

Connor laughed. "That poor kid. What a mouthful!"

"We know it's a long one," she explained, "but we don't care because we want him to appreciate his great heritage. Colin for Jarod's father, Matthew for the father you were to me, Matt, Ralph for his great-grandfather and Charlo for the father he was to Jarod after Colin died. Four men our son will grow up to revere."

With that announcement, Matt Henson's eyes filled.

And if Avery wasn't mistaken, Charlo's eyes went suspiciously bright, which was unusual for him.

"But we'll call him Cole." This from Jarod.

"Cole's a great name for a steer wrestler," Connor threw out, provoking chuckles.

Everyone got the chance to hold him. The baby was so good he didn't fuss, probably because of all the attention. Finally Avery let go of Zane's arm and walked over to Liz, who relinquished him with great reluctance.

Avery stared down at him. "Welcome to our world, Cole Bannock. I adore your name! We've been waiting a long time for you, sweetheart. I'm your aunt Avery and I already love you more than words can say."

She put him over her shoulder and patted his back. What would it be like to have a baby like this with Zane? The joy would be beyond belief. After a minute she kissed his cheeks and then handed him to Charlo, who was last to be given the privilege.

He lifted him in the air. "He'll be known as Sun in his Hair by our people."

Sun in his Hair. "That's perfect," she said to Sadie who nodded and was crying with happiness.

When he handed him back to his mother, Sadie smiled up at him. "We want him to learn from you, Uncle Charlo. He'll be the luckiest boy in the world."

"Sorry to intrude," the doctor spoke up. "Time to get the baby to the nursery and for Sadie to get her sleep."

They cleared the room and went into the lounge. Connor walked over to Avery and hugged her hard, lifting her off the ground before putting her down again.

"Now that we don't have to worry about Sits in the Center anymore, we all want to hear your news."

Avery blinked. "What are you talking about?"

He reached for her left hand and lifted it so everyone could see. He whistled and darted Zane a glance. "You don't find a ring like this in a Cracker Jack box."

Her body went hot, then cold, before a groan escaped her lips. When they got the call to go over to the hospital, she'd forgotten to take it off and put it in her purse. Now it was too late. Everyone could see it. Everyone knew who had given it to her.

She was afraid to look at Zane. He stood there without helping her out. Because she hadn't said no when he'd put it on her finger, she couldn't embarrass him by saying she'd just been trying it on and forgot to put it away. It wouldn't be the truth, nor would it be fair to him.

The room had gone as quiet as a tomb.

Sucking in her breath she said, "Zane gave me this ring tonight. But before I even had a chance to think, we heard the news about the baby and rushed over here. Since Grandpa has no idea what has happened, I'd appreciate it if none of you said anything.

"Zane and I have certain things to work out before any kind of an announcement can be made. If or when we do, I want Grandpa to be the first to know. I hope you'll understand. Tonight is Sadie and Jarod's night. Please let's keep it that way."

Connor eyed her speculatively before kissing her cheek. "Why don't we call Grandpa right now and tell him about Cole? Jarod has already talked to him, but he'll want to hear about him from us."

He pulled out his phone and rang him. When Ralph answered, Connor put it on speaker. "Hi, Grandpa. How does it feel to be a great-grandfather?"

"Wonderful!"

"Did Jarod tell you what they named him?"

"Cole."

"But that's not his legal name."

"What is it?"

"Colin Matthew Ralph Charlo Bannock."

Total silence came from the other end of the phone. Avery could only imagine her grandfather's joy.

"Charlo and Pauline are with us, Grandpa. He has given Cole the official name of Sun in his Hair."

They heard Ralph clear his throat. "Tell Charlo I approve."

So did Avery, but right now she wanted to leave the hospital. Zane hovered in the background, waiting to take her back to her truck. She was glad they wouldn't be driving to the ranch together.

She'd meant what she'd said. They had certain things to work out. What if she could never be a wife to him in the truest sense of the word? He said it didn't matter because she was the only woman he would ever love. But he couldn't know what he was saying.

She thought about how Zane didn't try to talk to her in that tension-filled moment when Connor had drawn everyone's attention to her ring. He'd let her handle it. Somehow he always knew what to do where she was concerned.

When they reached her truck, he told her he'd follow her home and get in touch with her tomorrow.

"Tomorrow I have a class on the reservation before I go to the dig site."

"I'll be in Billings part of the day, but we'll catch up with each other at some point. Drive home safely. I'll be behind you."

"Wait—" she said, but he'd already headed for his truck. They needed to talk more about this, but he didn't give her the chance.

Alone in the cab of her own truck, she headed for the ranch with her emotions in a turbulent state. She loved him so much but was scared to death to take the next step with him. The thought of ever losing him devastated her.

The moon beamed through the window, illuminating the diamond. It blinded her with its radiance. Zane had such faith in a future with her, he'd given her a ring tonight. And what did she do in response?

Virtually nothing. Worse, she'd downplayed it in front of her family. Avery despised herself and couldn't let it go like this.

When they reached the road that turned into her ranch, she kept going until she pulled up to the Corkin ranch house. Before she lost courage, she climbed out and walked up to the front door to wait for him.

BLOOD POUNDED IN his ears as Zane got out of the truck and hurried toward her. "What's wrong?"

"Can we go inside to talk for a minute?"

Was she going to give the ring back? Feeling sick,

he unlocked the door and showed her into the living room. Only the light from one lamp was on. "Do you want coffee? Or a soda?"

"No, thank you." They stood in front of each other almost like adversaries. It was insane when the total opposite was true. "I need to get this off my chest."

Zane grimaced, fearing the worst. "Go ahead."

"I've been awful to you all night," she said. "I'm so ashamed. You have to forgive me."

He shook his head. "You need to forgive me for giving you that ring when you weren't ready for it. I told you I was a patient man, but I lied."

She looked up at him. "Can we start over?"

His heart skipped a beat. "What do you mean?"

"Every girl dreams of the day when the man she loves asks her to marry him. I was a typical girl with all those dreams, but the assault turned me into something else. I saw myself in the mirror tonight when you gave me the ring and proposed to me. The ugly image staring back was the me I've become."

She rubbed her arms. "At the hospital, I saw myself in the mirror again. That hideous image was still there. I hate that image," she cried in a tremulous voice. "I want to go back to being the girl I once was. I want to be your wife. Take me in your arms and kiss me. Please, Zane."

"Darling," he murmured. In the next breath he cupped her face in his hands and lowered his mouth over hers. The first taste of her was to die for, but he was aware of her implicit trust in him and let her set the pace.

They experimented, giving each other kiss after kiss until gradually she wanted more and didn't pull away as their kisses grew longer and deeper. More than anything in the world he wanted to pull her close, but he didn't dare. Not being in her skin, he had no idea of the nightmare she'd been living with. Zane was operating without a guide. She had to be the one to let him know what she wanted.

He smothered a moan when she unexpectedly lifted her arms and wound them around his neck. Now their bodies were touching from head to toe. What to do with his hands that wouldn't send her back to that dark place?

"Hold me close," she begged. "I wanted to do this while we were dancing."

That helped him. Zane enfolded her the way he would have done at the hotel. "I love dancing with you." He started moving them around the room while still kissing her. "You're the perfect fit for me."

This was heaven to him. She smelled divine. Everything about her appealed to him. Avery was femininity personified.

She kissed the side of his jaw. "I love you, Zane, more than you can imagine. Tonight at the hospital it hit me just how much I wanted to shout it to the world, but I was afraid."

He kissed her hair. "What's happened since then?"

"On the drive home, I could see you through the rearview mirror. The closer we got to the ranch, the more I knew that I wanted to see you in my mirror whether coming, going or staying, for the rest of my life."

"I had the same vision watching you through my windshield. When you were holding Cole, I could see you holding a child of ours."

"So could I," she admitted in a trembling voice. "If you can put up with me, I'll marry you and never take off this gorgeous ring. Grandpa will probably plan a party on Sunday evening to celebrate the baby. We can announce our news then."

He stopped dancing and clasped her shoulders. "How soon do you want to set a date?"

Unwavering gray eyes stared up at him. "As soon as possible."

"You mean that? Honestly?"

She nodded. "How about July 17? Sadie's original due date. The dig site project will be finished by then. It will give us a three-day weekend if you can arrange to take the time off from work before the following Monday."

Avery was ruling out a long honeymoon, but that didn't matter. "Where?"

"At our church, where Connor and Liz were married, but only if that's all right with you."

"How can you even ask?"

"Just checking."

"Nedra and I got married at a courthouse. It wasn't the kind of wedding I wanted, but because of time constraints, it was the only way."

"I'm so sorry," she said.

"Don't be. That's all in the past. My marriage to

you is going to be an entirely different proposition in every way."

She stood on tiptoe to kiss his mouth. "Our marriage is going to be the one I always wanted. I've loved you for a whole year, Zane Lawson. Never having been close with you like this before has been agony for me. You never tried to kiss me."

"I didn't want to scare you off."

"Well, it had the opposite effect." Now she told him, "I don't want to wait any longer. If we contact the pastor right away, there shouldn't be any problem."

Zane kissed her long and hard again before letting her go, unable to believe this was really happening. "I'll make you a promise. Being able to kiss and hold you like this is enough for me. After we're married we'll ease into making love, but only when you're ready."

She started to say something, but he put a finger to her lips. "Don't tell me that you might never be ready. If that day comes, then we'll deal with it and go for more counseling. Knowing that both of us have been living with PTSD for a long time, the fact that we love each other and want to live together now is a gift I hadn't expected this soon."

A smile lifted the corner of her enticing mouth. "I wasn't going to tell you that. Just the opposite in fact."

Avery was trying to be brave and he adored her for it, but he'd read the pamphlet and knew this was not going to be an easy journey for her. She might wake up before morning and regret everything she'd said. According to Dr. Lindstrom, Zane wouldn't find this an easy path, either. But tonight his heart was singing.

He kissed her cheek. "We have exactly three weeks to plan everything."

"We'll have the reception at the ranch. By then Sadie will be on her feet again. I'll ask Cassie to be my matron of honor."

"Do you think Jarod would do the honors for me?"

"You're fishing again, alien," she teased. "He wouldn't let anyone else."

Zane wanted to carry her to the couch and hold her for the rest of the night. It took all the self-control he possessed to let her decide where they went from here. "Do you have some kind of theme in mind?"

"Do you?" she countered.

"No. The men I know don't care about things like that. It's up to the ladies."

She laughed. "Well, this lady just wants a plain old Western wedding, done Bannock-style."

He pressed his forehead against hers. "That's another reason I love you so much. I'm crazy in love with you, you know that."

When he embraced her this time, the desire that had been smoldering burst into flame. He was terrified that he was getting too close to the line, another minute and he could make a fatal mistake with her without realizing it. Before he demolished the groundwork he'd prepared so carefully, he stepped away and slid his hands down her arms.

The diamond winked at him in the dim light. He reached for her hand and kissed the palm. Glancing at her he said, "You've made me the happiest man alive tonight. In three weeks I won't have to follow you back to your house."

She took a quick breath. "I can't wait."

"Shall we go?" he asked when it was the last thing he wanted to do. "No doubt Ralph is still up and dying to talk to you about the baby."

"Liz and Connor are probably there. Jarod has been tied up in knots for months with worry. We all need a break from it."

Zane chuckled as he walked her out of the house to her truck. "Now that he has little Cole to help take care of, he'll be too tired to worry."

Avery climbed in behind the wheel. Zane shut the door. She turned to him with a smile that was like pure sunshine to him. "A happy kind of tired. Finally. Thank heaven Uncle Charlo showed up when he did or I don't think my brother would've made it."

He leaned inside and kissed her with mounting passion. It was a good thing the door kept them apart. They were both breathing hard when he eventually let her go. "I'll call you tomorrow."

Her flushed face was the last thing he saw before she backed out. He climbed in his truck and followed her home. Sure enough, Connor's truck was out in front. Zane left the headlights on as she hurried to the front door and waved. "Good night, sweetheart."

Good night, sweetheart.

To hear those words come out of her was a pure miracle.

Filled with energy, Zane knew he couldn't sleep yet. After he got home, he sat down at the computer and saw some interesting information. First of all, one of the agents at the BLM in Helena had checked out Steve Newell and learned that the guy had withdrawn from summer school in Missoula, and no one knew where he was. The date of his withdrawal was a few days before the dynamite heist. Zane told the agent to put out an APB on Steve's Toyota.

The second piece of information was mind-blowing. The traces of dirt from the ATV and Terry Newell's car treads were a match for the soil at the Absarokee site. This was enough for Zane to go on and arrest them in the morning. While in Billings, he'd run by the federal storage facility where the dynamite had been stolen. Hopefully by tomorrow afternoon he'd hear back about the samples where the explosion had occurred up on the mountain.

He printed off pictures of the Newell boys' IDs and put them in his wallet. After he visited the Newell ranch again with the warrant, he'd use the pictures when he visited some shops in Billings and smaller towns like Absarokee that sold cutters and detonation cord. The boys had to pick up the materials from somewhere. Someone would recognize their photos.

To clean up this case soon was a top priority. He wanted it sorted out before he married the woman he adored.

FRIDAY AFTERNOON AVERY was working at the dig site when a familiar figure approached. She looked up from the sorting tray and smiled. "Tom—it's so nice to see you again. Where's Smiling Face?"

Tom Medicinehorse was one of the tribal monitors from the Pryor reservation who'd been checking on their progress at the dig site, but today he wore a solemn expression that worried her. No doubt the vandalism was the topic of concern at Crow Agency.

He usually brought his adorable eight-year-old son with him. Avery just loved that boy. He was smart and taught her new words every time he came. She in turn plied him with stories she'd been learning from Long Hair.

There wasn't a child in the world who didn't love to hear a good tale, but Smiling Face had a natural curiosity and never wanted her to stop. Often his father had to drag him home so she could get on with her work. Of course she didn't mind his company. He was so entertaining she was crazy about him and told his father as much.

Tom stared at her with eyes black as pitch. "Smiling Face is missing."

Avery swallowed with difficulty. If his father said the boy was missing, then he was *really* missing because those on the reservation would have been out looking for him.

"For how long?"

"This morning he couldn't be found. Everyone has been searching."

School was out. It meant he'd left his house before anyone noticed. She didn't know what to say, but felt sick inside for Tom and his wife who had two other children and had to be frantic. "He hasn't been here while I've been working."

"Charlo says you can find him."

The comment stunned her. "You've seen Charlo today?" He nodded. "Did he give you a reason why he thought I would know anything?"

He nodded again. "He told me to tell you he had a dream about the Little People."

The Little People?

As recognition dawned, a small cry escaped her lips. She knew exactly what Charlo meant.

Smiling Face loved the stories about the Little People who lived on Pryor Mountain near the Medicine Wheel. She'd been recording those stories for the past two years. The boy wanted a peek at them and had begged Avery to help him find one.

She would laugh and tell him they were too quick to be caught. There were several traditions about the Little People in the Crow culture. The one he liked best said they were fun-loving, mischievous little men and women. They helped the Crow out when they were needed, but otherwise were blamed for things going missing and other upsets at home. They didn't resemble the Apsaalooké. In ancient days they were little white folks who could be seen now and then.

Now that he'd turned eight, he felt old enough to go in search of them on his own, but it was a long way without transportation. If he knew someone was traveling to the mountains, he might have hidden in the back of their pickup truck. But he'd been gone all day and could be lost. It broke her heart to think he might be up there alone and defenseless. His poor parents.

Avery had no choice but to go. She *wanted* to. In

one respect she felt responsible because she'd probably indulged him too much with the stories she told him.

"I'll leave for the ranch now to get my horse." She pulled the cell phone out of her pocket. "Tell me your number so I can stay in contact with you."

They exchanged phone numbers.

"If he's where I think he is, then I'll find him, Tom."

He stared at her. "Thank you."

She would have told him not to worry, but that was absurd. When a child went missing, everyone was worried. As he walked toward his truck, she ran through the grass to Dr. Osgood and told him what had happened.

The professor urged her to leave immediately. "The site will still be here in the morning. We hope," he added. The dark humor made her laugh before she headed for her truck. On the way home she phoned Rusty, the stable manager on the Bannock ranch. She asked him to hitch up the small horse trailer to the blue truck, the one with the spotlights mounted on the roof. She also asked that he put Snowball inside with all her gear.

Next she called their housekeeper, Jenny, and found out her grandfather was with Connor. Avery left word where she was going and why, but she also needed a favor and asked Jenny to fix a hamper with enough food to last two people twenty-four hours. It didn't take long before she reached the ranch.

Avery packed up a couple of sleeping bags and blankets, then did her own packing. Before leaving, she loaded some lanterns and flashlights in the back in order to be prepared. She would call Zane later.

He was out on an important case and she hated disturbing him. Maybe she'd hear from him when he was finished for the day, but right now time was of the essence to find Smiling Face. It was four o'clock. By the time she reached the cave area on Pryor Mountain, it would be five. That would give her four hours of daylight to search the area on horseback.

Two hours later, she'd ridden Snowball to the opening of a limestone crevice where hundreds of piles of rocks had been placed by the Apsaalooké tribe for their sacred spot. This was the place of spiritual fasting where the Little People lived under the ground and passed between their home and the upper air. Their destination was the Medicine Wheel.

Throughout the plains of Alberta, Saskatchewan, Montana, the Dakotas and Wyoming there were over a hundred archaeological features called Medicine Wheels. Avery had traveled to many of them. Most were constructed long before the first Europeans entered the region.

This Medicine Wheel on Pryor Mountain had U-shaped stone features associated with the vision quest. The person seeking a vision would have interaction with the Little People. The stones were arranged in lines as living symbols.

Darkness was descending as Avery dismounted and climbed up on one of the tallest clumps of rocks to shout the missing boy's name. There were more Medicine Wheels in the distance, but she didn't dare go any farther this close to dark. She must have called out his name twenty times over the past half an hour.

Her fear was that he'd gone into the cave and had become lost. The little guy had to be frightened and hungry. All she could do was camp outside the opening with the lights on and call to him every so often to let him know he wasn't alone.

After she'd fed and watered Snowball, she led her back into the trailer and shut the door. Then she got in the truck and discovered two messages waiting for her. The first was from Tom who had no news to report yet but was bringing help. She called him back and gave him her location. She would keep watch tonight and urged him not to lose hope.

The next message was from Connor who was angrier than she'd ever heard him because he knew she was alone and it had upset Ralph. He and Liz were on their way to help in the search. Their grandfather suggested they take the razor-backed road in case Smiling Face chose that trail to reach the Medicine Wheel. They'd stay in close touch.

Just then Zane phoned. On cue she felt an adrenaline surge and picked up. "Zane? Are you through with work?"

"I'm pulling up to the ranch now. Where are you?"

Just hearing his deep voice made her toes curl. When she told him her location and why she was up there, a strange sound escaped his throat. He was as upset as Connor, but tried to conceal it without much success. She loved him for it.

"Connor and Liz are on their way up, too, via the razor-backed road. Call them and let them know you're coming. It'll calm him down."

"I will. Give me your exact coordinates. I'm leaving now."

Avery gave him instructions. "When you reach the rocks near the top of Pryor Mountain road, you won't be able to miss me. I'll honk the horn and I've got the spotlights on full blast. I'm hoping Smiling Face will see them."

"We'll all pray for that, but please tell me you're locked in the cab."

"Of course. I've got my pistol, remember."

"Avery—" His voice sounded husky. "It was only last night you agreed to marry me. Now I hear you're up in the mountains alone." His vulnerability was a revelation.

"I know this area like the back of my hand. It's a sacred place. Nothing's going to happen to me."

"Stay on the phone with me anyway. I've a lot to tell you."

"I want to hear it, but give me a few minutes while I shout to Smiling Face one more time. Then I'll call you back and stay on the phone with you as long as I can. Unfortunately my battery is low and I forgot to bring the charger."

"In that case, save the battery for an emergency. I'll tell you everything when I get there."

"I know you drive fast, but don't take any unnecessary risks. I couldn't handle it if you got into an accident."

"Now you know how I feel," he said. "Don't take any chances, Avery." He clicked off.

Chapter Nine

Knowing Zane was on his way filled her with warmth. She undid the lock and climbed out of the cab. After walking over to the cave opening she called to Smiling Face again, then she started back to the truck. Out of the corner of her eye she saw headlights coming and got inside the cab to lock the doors. In a minute Zane's truck pulled up alongside her. They both got out at the same time and she ran into his arms.

"Thank God you're safe," he said in an unsteady voice against her neck. "You were easy to find. This spot is lit up like a Christmas tree, but I take it there's no sign of Smiling Face yet."

She clasped him tighter. "No, but I'm positive he's in the cave."

"Why do you think that?"

Avery told him about Charlo's dream. "The Little People live inside this cave."

"Tell me about them."

After she explained she said, "I believe this is where he came hoping to find them. If he has a concussion, maybe he can still hear my voice. I've been talking to him and telling him stories just in case."

Zane cradled her face. His loving blue eyes traveled over each feature before he kissed her. "I have no doubt that boy has heard you. We'll find him. Connor's trailing their horses. They'll do a thorough search at the top of the razor-backed road, then he'll wind around and meet up with us."

Their mouths clung for moment before he lifted his. "It's cooling off. Why don't you get in your truck while I go inside the cave and call to him for a while."

She stared up at him. "I love you, Zane. I'm so happy you're here."

A breeze had sprung up. He smoothed a strand of hair away from her eyes. "I wouldn't be anywhere else."

They walked back to her truck. She handed him the big flashlight. "Don't go in too far. Promise me."

"Don't worry," he said against her lips, then made his way to the cave opening. She shivered when he disappeared inside.

At first she could hear his voice through the open window of the truck. Then it grew fainter until there was no sound at all except the breeze rustling the underbrush. When she couldn't stand it any longer, she got out and ran to the cave opening.

"Zane?"

In a minute she heard him call to her. "I'm coming."

"Did you see a sign of anything?"

Suddenly he appeared. "I found this at a bifurcation in the cave."

A cry of excitement escaped her lips. "This is his

little buffalo medicine bundle. He's here! This is really precious to him. I know there's a small knife made from a buffalo bone inside, but I don't dare open it."

"Why?"

"Smiling Face keeps this sacred talisman in remembrance of the buffalo. It's not for me to open.

"Chief Plenty Coups said that when the buffalo went away, the Crow became a changed people. When the buffalo was with them, they were never idle, but after they were gone, everything was stolen from their minds and bodies. His people fell to the ground, and they could not lift themselves up again. Smiling Face refuses to fall down."

She saw Zane's throat working. "To have such a strong ethic at his young age is humbling."

"He's a special boy. I love him. He must have taken a wrong turn and could have fallen, possibly knocking himself out."

Zane put his arm around her shoulders. "We'll find him in the morning."

"I need to phone Tom. This will give him hope." For the next few minutes they talked. When she hung up she told Zane that Tom would be there soon with some of the men and they'd form a line.

"He has to be so grateful to you." They moved to her truck where she put the bundle on the backseat. Zane looked all around. "It's a magical night. Shall we sleep in the back where we can hear sounds?"

"I was hoping you'd say that. I brought two sleeping bags and plenty of food."

"Keep your phone handy in case he calls."

Together they got everything set up. Zane checked on Snowball, and then climbed inside the back next to her, against the side. At this altitude the stars glittered in the sky. They ate sandwiches and fruit. Jenny had packed sodas and bottled water.

The two of them lacked for nothing. Tonight she refused to let that black place inside her take up any room. Despite the fact that they hadn't found Smiling Face yet, she'd never been so happy and content in her life.

Zane had come to her world from a completely different life, yet nestled against him, it felt as if he'd always been a part of hers. His prophecy came to mind once more.

"God long ago drew a circle in the sand exactly around the spot where you are standing right now. I was never not coming here. This was never not going to happen."

When her cell phone rang, it pierced the quiet of the night, causing her to jerk straight up. She checked the caller ID and answered. "Connor?"

"Avery, have you seen any sign of Tom's son yet?"

"A sign, yes. Zane went in the cave and found his medicine bundle. He's in there somewhere."

"I've spoken to Tom. He's bringing help now. Liz and I hope to be there soon, but my right rear tire has gone flat. When I get it repaired, we'll come. We've brought our horses."

"Good. Call me when you're almost here and I'll turn the truck spotlights back on."

"Will do. Let me talk to Zane for a minute."

While the men spoke, she put things back in the hamper. After he ended the call with Connor, she stood up and called to Smiling Face one more time.

"We're right here in front of the cave. Stay strong. We'll find you in the morning."

Zane pulled her down onto his lap. He kissed her wet cheeks and held her as he would a child. Avery wept for a little while.

"What is it?"

"I'm trying to be positive, but as you know, black bears are abundant here because of the forage. This cave is a perfect hibernating spot."

He tightened his arms around her. "It's not the season. Even if a bear lives in there, it's probably out hunting. And I'm sure Tom's boy has been taught what to do if he encounters one."

"I know. I have to have faith." She kissed his chin. "On the phone you said you had news about the case."

"It's breaking wide-open. I've identified one of the vandals, a twenty-one-year-old son of a rancher. His name's Terry Newell. The family's from Laurel."

She sat up. "You don't mean Lester Newell—"

He blinked. "Yes, why? You know him?"

"He's one of the spokesmen for the Carbon County Cattlemen's Association. I can't believe he has a son who could do anything so evil."

Zane's brows lifted. "Two sons, Terry and Steve. There's an APB out on the oldest son, too. He's supposedly been away at school in Missoula."

"You're not serious."

"I'm afraid so. The evidence puts their vehicles at

the vision quest site, the recreation area, your dig site and probably countless others. It's possible they're responsible for stealing all that dynamite from the forest service shed. I've got a hunch we'll find more traces of it in the other brother's car."

She shook her head. "This is shocking. My grandfather is friends with him."

"Maybe the father doesn't know anything. After I returned to the Newell ranch with the warrant, I found a small cache of dynamite in a trailer on the property. If it's part of the same dynamite taken during the heist, then our office will close in and make arrests."

"That's so incredibly awful."

"I'm inclined to think others are involved. Before I left Laurel, I talked to a café owner who identified the one son from the photo I showed him. He often eats there. Lately he's been joined by a man driving a BIA truck."

"What?" Her thoughts reeled.

"Perhaps the BIA is conducting its own investigation. If it's Durant, maybe because of a lead on the stolen artifacts he was transferred here from Nebraska to investigate. The timing's about right."

"Do you think he might have been tailing the son the night we went into the bar?"

"I don't know."

She looked into his eyes. "What aren't you telling me?"

Zane studied her for a moment. "I'm not sure."

"But you've got an idea."

"Lots of them." Something had bothered him about

Durant from the beginning, but he didn't want to alarm Avery. He brushed his mouth against hers. "Right now I want to walk over to the cave opening and try to make contact with Smiling Face one more time."

Avery moved so he could stand up. He jumped out with the flashlight and walked inside the cave a little way, calling out, then waited in case there was an answer. After a dozen tries he returned to the truck. "No response," he murmured to her before putting the hamper in the bear locker for the rest of the night.

"Why don't you climb in your sleeping bag and try to sleep. I'll take the first watch and wait up for Connor." He was longing for the time when they'd get in a sleeping bag together.

"I won't be able to sleep. We'll do this together."

"Then come here to me." He reached for her once more and put her sleeping bag around their legs. "We have a lot to talk about. I want to know what your plans are after you've finished work at the dig site. Won't it be over soon?"

"Yes. I've accepted a teaching position at Montana State in Billings. It's a one-year contract teaching Native American studies."

"When does it start?"

"September. I'll be teaching three classes, two in the mornings on Monday, Wednesday and Friday, and a three-hour evening class on Thursday. Until it starts, I plan to keep working on the reservation while I gather more stories for my book."

He pulled her closer. "That sounds perfect. I'll drive

you on Thursdays and put in some work at the field office. When you're through, we'll make a night of it."

She burrowed her face in his shoulder. "When you talk like this, it makes life sound wonderful and—normal." He heard the little catch in her voice before she cried quietly. Her tears tore him apart. No power on earth could erase that horrible experience from her mind, or his.

All Zane could do was keep remembering what the doctor said. *Show your unconditional love and support.* He wished they were getting married in the morning. As her husband, he could be there for her whenever she broke down. He held her for a long time.

The thought of what that pervert had done to her filled him with rage. He had to fight to tamp it down. It didn't help his state of mind or hers that they hadn't found Smiling Face yet. His fear for the boy's safety combined with his suspicion that Mike Durant might not be squeaky clean caused him to bite down hard.

His phone rang, bringing his tortured thoughts to a halt. Avery stirred as he answered. "Connor?"

"Yup. We're close to you now."

"Honk your horn while I turn on the spotlights. The sound will carry a long way. Hopefully the boy's in a condition to hear it so he won't lose hope."

"Good idea."

Soon after Zane had the lights back on, they heard the blare of Connor's truck horn. Avery got to her feet and jumped down. "I need to check on Snowball so she won't be nervous."

She opened the trailer door. "It's okay, Snowball."

Her horse nickered loudly when she approached. "We have company." She gentled her animal. Liz soon joined her. "Well, look who's here—your favorite vet."

The two women hugged. "How are you doing, Snowball? Did that horn frighten you? It would have done the same thing to me. After all, it's four in the morning." Liz pulled a treat out of her pocket and fed it to the horse. Snowball chomped it down.

"Connor phoned Tom. A lot of help is coming this way. We ought to be able to penetrate deep into the cave as soon as they get here. It won't be long before we find him. Zane told us everything. Because of you they know where to come."

"It's true. Oh, Liz, I feel so guilty about it."

"Why? You can't help it that Smiling Face wanted to find the Little People. He's a kid with a big imagination."

"You're right."

"Jarod wanted to come, but he can't leave Sadie yet."

"Of course not. If you're hungry, there's food in the bear locker."

"Don't worry about us. We brought enough for a dozen people, just in case." She grasped Avery's hand to look at the ring. "Have you and Zane come to any decisions?"

She nodded. "We're going to be married in three weeks."

With a cry, Liz's arms went around her in a bear hug. She wasn't a barrel racer for nothing. "I think every dream of mine has now come true. He's madly in love with you, as if you didn't know. I already knew how you felt about him at the funeral."

"You couldn't have. We didn't know each other."

"I saw the way you looked at him during the reception. When he looked back at you, it was a magical moment. I've never seen love at first sight happen before and it blew me away. Charlo would say it was written in the stars."

Avery averted her eyes. "Charlo sees everything."

Liz shivered. "I know that for a fact. Which means he knows Smiling Face will be found."

She lifted her head. "You're right." While she rubbed her horse's forelock they heard sounds of other vehicles coming. "It sounds like help has arrived, Snowball. I'll be back in a while."

They left the trailer in time to see four truckloads of men from the reservation jump down. Tom walked up to Avery. *"Kahee,"* he greeted her.

"Kahee." She took him over to her truck and handed him the little buffalo bundle. "I haven't opened it. We're going to find him, Tom."

He gave her a solemn nod before going back to his truck. In the meantime the men had formed a line with rope and started into the cave with their flashlights. Zane hurried over to her. "Connor has gone ahead. I'm going to go in with them. You and Liz stay here. Lock yourselves in the cab."

"We promise. Be careful."

"Always." He gave her a swift kiss before everyone disappeared inside the dark hole.

The waiting game had begun. Liz needed to check

on their horses. Avery went with her, and then they got in Avery's truck. For the next hour she and Liz talked about the wedding plans.

"I *knew* Zane was the reason you haven't wanted to date." Liz had that part right. Zane was the only man she'd ever loved. But the other part she didn't want to think about right now.

"I love him with all my heart, Liz."

"Thank goodness he was transferred back here. My parents are going to shout for joy when they hear you're engaged. Zane's becoming the son mom and dad never had."

"I know. Grandpa loves him, too."

"You can say that again."

They waited for the men. When dawn crept over the mountain and they still hadn't come out, Avery got a sick feeling inside.

"Liz, if you don't mind staying here, I'm going to saddle Snowball and go up to those rocks again. I've been thinking about his bundle. If he'd been knocked unconscious, his body would have been next to it. What if he's not inside? Maybe there's a reason he left the cave without it. He could have thought the tunnel came out the other side of the rocks. I'm going to go look around. Will you be all right?"

"You're asking me that? I've been going alone into the mountains early in the morning for years to train my horses."

Avery smiled at her friend, grabbed some food and drinks from the hamper and put them in a saddlebag.

Liz walked to the trailer with her. In a few minutes Liz was ready. "I'll see you soon."

"If they've found Smiling Face, I'll ask Zane to shoot his gun so you'll know."

"Thanks. You're an angel."

Avery took off in the same direction as last night, calling his name every few yards. But this time she wound around to the other side and down into a small gully filled with clumps of pine trees. The terrain was rocky and uneven.

She'd been gone ten minutes. At the base of one tree, she halted to give Snowball a rest. Charlo had sent Tom to her. This morning she felt the earth and the heavens were closely aligned and knew they would find the little boy if they just kept looking.

She was about ready to move on when several pine cones dropped on her head. Avery looked up in surprise and saw something huddled in the upper branches. *"Smiling Face?"* Her heart was beating fast. "Is that you?"

A little moaning sound came back.

"I'm coming!" She dismounted and climbed the tree. The boy was lying along a limb with cuts on his arm and the side of his face. His features were pale. "You poor darling."

She reached for him and put him in a fireman's lift while she carried him to the ground. He was exhausted. After laying him down on the ground, she hurried over to the saddlebag for water. He drank thirstily. As she was feeding him one of the sandwiches, she heard someone coming full speed toward them on a horse.

Avery looked behind her. "Zane!" Her heart always thrilled to see him. "I've found him!"

He hit the ground with Connor's horse still running and dashed over to her and the boy.

"Those look like bear slashes, but the blood has dried."

Smiling Face nodded. "In the cave. I ran up here to get away."

Avery smoothed his black hair. "You did exactly the right thing."

"We're proud of you," Zane told him. "Your father is waiting for you at the entrance to the cave. Do you think you can sit on my horse?"

"Yes."

She rounded up Lightning and led him over to Snowball. Zane lifted the boy and climbed in the saddle behind him. Avery mounted her horse and the two of them headed back toward the cave with their precious cargo.

"Smiling Face, I'm going to shoot my gun so everyone knows you've been found. Is that okay with you, son?"

The boy nodded.

Zane reached for his gun and fired two shots.

"Smiling Face?" she said. "I know you were out here trying to find the Little People's home. I'm sorry you got hurt, but don't worry. The Great Spirit knows you were very, very brave to stay out here all night and He has kept you safe.

"Remember the words of Chief Plenty Coups? 'The ground on which you stand is sacred. It is the blood of your ancestors and you will be protected.' One day you will grow into a great warrior, Smiling Face, and will tell your children how you found the home of the Little People and how they protected you from the bear."

She leaned sideways to pat his leg. "Do you remember the story I told you about the child who fell from a travois and was cared for by the Little People? They made the stone arrow points in this canyon. Though small, they were strong and carried buffalo on their backs."

"I remember."

"Well, that boy stayed with them until he became a man of superhuman strength. Is that why you came up here? Did you want to pray for the same strength as the Little People's? You're a very noble boy and your parents are very proud of you. Today you will return with your father and tell them your story."

"The bear took my bundle."

"But he dropped it. I found it and gave it to your father. That bundle protected you."

Zane flashed her a tender look that melted her insides. They made fast time. Tom was there at the head of the others as they approached the cave entrance. The reunion between father and son was something she'd remember all her life. He lifted his son off the horse and clasped him to his heart.

Tom's eyes stared at Avery over his boy's dark head. "Many thanks to you, Winter Fire Woman."

Winter Fire Woman?

She eyed Zane, who looked equally mystified by the

comment. Jarod would know what Tom meant. She'd have to ask him later.

"You're welcome. I'll come to see Smiling Face when he's able to tell you how the Little People gave him courage."

"Aho," the boy thanked her.

In a few minutes everyone had gone, even Connor and Liz. Zane helped her put Snowball back in the trailer. When they shut the door, he reached for her shoulders. "You have more courage than anyone I've ever known. Maybe Tom's name for you is a metaphor for that."

His words touched her. She traced an index finger over his lips. "I don't know about that. Without your help—"

"You came for him by yourself," he interrupted her. His mouth drew closer. After the happy resolution of the past twelve hours, Avery's exhilaration made her hungry for his kiss.

She held on to him, loving this man who'd become her life. How had she existed all these years without him?

"Let's get in the back of the truck for a while and enjoy this wonderful morning."

Feeling as though she'd been caught up in a dream, she climbed in with him. He laid the sleeping bags side by side and drew her down with him. The sun's rays shot pale yellow and orange across the sky, not high enough to reach inside the truck yet, but they provided a heavenly panorama above their heads.

Wherever his blue eyes touched, they lit fires. "I

love you, Avery. With you as my wife, I feel I could
do anything. When the day comes, you will be the best
mother a child could ever have."

And he would be the best father. She kissed him
with growing hunger. He was a beautiful man. She
could study him for hours. With those hard-boned features and his rip-cord physique, he was male through
and through. To the enemy he would look severe while
he was in pursuit. But Avery knew his other side. When
he smiled, those dimples reduced her to a liquefied
state.

"Zane—" she murmured with growing desire, needing to be closer still. But the second he reached across
to roll her against him, she found herself in a black,
horrifying place. Suppressing a cry, she scrambled out
of his reach.

"It's okay, Avery. It's Zane. You're with me, darling. You're safe." He sat there looking up at her with
wounded eyes.

Her legs leaned against the bear locker. Between
shaking and breathing so hard, she came close to hy-
perventilating. It took a minute before she was able to
talk. "I'm sorry. I'm so sorry."

He stayed where he was with his legs upraised.
"Don't say it. What happened just now was no one's
fault. You had a flashback. Why don't you get us a soda
out of the locker? Then I'd like you to sit down on top
of it and we'll talk about expectations. Yours and mine.
How does that sound?"

"I've hurt you again."

"Not this time because we knew you'd have a flashback at some point."

"This is what I've been afraid of."

"Your courage helped find a little boy this morning. That same courage is going to get you through this and I'm going to be here for you."

No one was more wonderful than Zane. She found them each a drink and then sat down as he'd suggested.

"You were with me until I did what?"

She threw her head back, closing her eyes. "Your arm started to roll me into you and suddenly I wasn't with you anymore."

"That's probably because we were lying down. Until that point you enjoyed kissing and holding me, right?"

"You know I did."

"Then that's huge progress you've made. This morning we've learned that we won't be lying on a bed, a truck bed, a couch or grass unless you feel ready for that step. You'll have to be the one to tell me."

She moaned. "It sounds so awful, like we're working from a blueprint."

"That's exactly what we're doing. You were taken by surprise. I don't want to spring another surprise on you that sets you off."

"But—"

"No buts," he silenced her. "I've been in heaven kissing you. I could go on doing it forever. In time you may find you want more and then we'll talk about what you want. I'll let you know what I'm planning to do before we do anything. You'll be able to decide what will work for you and if you can handle it. The more knowledge you have ahead of time lowers the chance of another flashback coming on."

Avery opened her eyes to look at him. "How do you know so much?"

"I don't. My doctor gave me a pamphlet geared for partners of assault victims. Otherwise I'd be operating blind."

She pressed her hands together. "It shouldn't have to be this way—"

"Lots of things shouldn't have to be the way they are, but that's life. One night, or even one day when I'm asleep, I'll be having a nightmare and you'll be shocked by what you see and hear. I'm afraid the first time will frighten you.

"Be assured I'll get over it, but don't try to wake me up. If you touch me while I'm in my dream, I'll think you're the enemy. Just give me my space until I come out of it and realize where I am."

Her eyes clouded over. "You poor thing."

"That's how I felt about you a little while ago. We're both wounded, but we're warriors, right?" He flashed her one of those Lawson smiles that lit up her universe.

"Yes, sweetheart." She got up from the locker and knelt down to throw her arms around his neck. He'd suffered so much, she found herself pressing kisses all over his face and neck. "I'm so in love with you, Zane. Please don't give up on me."

"It'll never happen," he whispered against her lips. Before she knew it, she'd climbed into his lap and was kissing him with a hunger she didn't know herself capable of. He let her do all the work. What woman had ever been blessed with a better man? His self-control was as astounding as his selflessness. But the heat of his response was growing along with hers. She knew it was time for her to stop. Slowly she relinquished his mouth. "I'm not being fair to you."

"Don't go away yet," he begged.

They kissed one more time long and hard before she stood up. "We need food. I'll get it for us."

They ate sandwiches and fruit. He finished off some cookies and packed the locker while she jumped out to check on Snowball. Then she walked over to him. "Ready to go?"

"When you are. I'll follow you."

Avery wished they could be together for the drive home. Since their talk while they'd spent the day at the Medicine Wheel, she felt closer to him than ever. On impulse she cupped his face in her hands and stood on tiptoe to kiss him. "I wish we could talk on the phone on the way, but mine is about ready to die."

"I'll try to stand it until we reach White Lodge. I need to gas up."

"So do I. See you at Preston's."

"Where more kisses will continue," he teased and copped another one before climbing into his truck. She got in hers and they took off. How did she ever exist without him?

Chapter Ten

Zane stayed behind Avery and listened to the messages that had come in on his phone. Steve Newell's whereabouts were still unaccounted for, but he'd be found sooner or later. The crime lab had come back with a match on the dynamite. All the evidence was forming part of the same piece. Hopefully he'd be found soon. Zane would move in and arrests would be made.

His next message from Matt came as a blow. Someone had taken a shot at him when he was up in the pasture. It barely missed hitting him and killed the calf he'd been holding. Was it the stray bullet of a hunter too drunk to see what he was aiming at?

Zane didn't think so. Neither did Matt who felt it had been deliberate. They talked it over and decided the bullet had been meant for Zane. The two of them both wore the same color cowboy hat. Someone knew he was getting close to making an arrest and thought they'd take out the BLM agent who was making trouble. To Zane's horror, they'd almost killed Matt.

Since there'd been no arrests yet, Zane could see it being the Newell boys. However there was another person who knew from Avery that Zane had been assigned to the Billings office.

Mike Durant.

Was he the dirty BIA agent working with other agents across state lines? Were they the enablers who were part of a ring that stretched throughout the High Plains? The rise of artifact thefts was staggering. Was that what this was about? Payback time for Zane because Durant wasn't only jealous, but thwarted?

Though still young, Avery was becoming a noted archaeologist among the Crow. If Durant had tried to cozy up to her to get valuable information about other sites loaded with artifacts, he had to hate Zane for wrecking his con.

Durant knew Zane lived next door to the Bannock ranch. If he was involved in the run of heists to steal artifacts, then some of his helpers might well be the Newell brothers. Zane could be wrong about that and their actions could be unrelated, but he sure as hell intended to find out and would follow every lead no matter how sketchy. He texted Matt and told him to keep this under his hat until they talked in the morning.

Though tomorrow was Sunday, this was important enough to run by Sanders, the lead ranger. He called him and told him about the shooting. Zane wanted to make sure he had all the backup he needed when it came time to go in.

After a decent sleep there was going to be a party at the Bannock ranch to celebrate little Cole's birth. Zane wondered how Avery planned to inform her grandfather about their news. With his blessing they could go ahead with plans.

By the time he drove in and got to bed, he was physically exhausted, but his mind wouldn't turn off. He was glad the incident with Avery had happened. It had given him a chance to talk to her about the intimate side of their marriage. Until now they'd only tiptoed around it.

The information the doctor had given him was pure gold. Without it he would have floundered in agony after having frightened her. Thankfully she'd recovered enough to go back to his arms.

During those hours in the trailer when he'd felt her pistol and knew she'd been assaulted, he didn't see how they were ever going to pull themselves out of the blackness she had to live with.

Zane wasn't naive enough to believe that they could weather each storm as easily as the one earlier that morning. But it gave him hope.

ON SUNDAY EVENING A collective "aw" rang from the crowd on the terrace of the Bannock ranch when Sadie held up the baby. He was his own adorable person. Though born early he weighed seven pounds, two ounces and was twenty-two inches long. He had a little bit of his mom and his dad in him.

Avery had helped the cook and housekeeper set up a buffet table. Small tables were arranged around it. She felt feverish with longing while she waited for Zane to arrive as she watched her friends and family.

Jarod's uncle Charlo had come with his whole family. A happy-looking Jarod held Ryan. He walked around with him, chatting with Grant and his wife. Their son Ned was noticeably absent.

Their daughter Cassie and Logan came with the vet Sam Rafferty and stood talking with Connor and Liz. Ralph's brother Tyson sat next to him on the swing while his wife, Winnifred, chatted with Sadie and held Cole. Sadie, dressed in soft lemon yellow, looked fabulous for someone who'd just had a baby. Though she complained she had pounds to lose, Avery couldn't see where she'd put them. Mother and son were both golden blond. Sadie's eyes shone like sapphires.

Cole's eyes were muddy. Avery had a feeling he'd probably inherited Jarod's eyes. No one had eyes quite like his, so black and penetrating. What a contrast that would be with his fair hair when Cole grew to adulthood.

This was a thrilling night. If it weren't for Zane, Avery would be like a lost child looking through a store window, wanting all the things inside, but never being able to have them. When she thought about it too much, she felt a little bit of sickness creep in to imagine her life without him.

When she thought she couldn't stand it another second if he didn't show up soon, Millie and Matt came around the side with him. He was wearing jeans and a black Western shirt along with his cowboy hat. A year ago he would have come in a suit and tie. She loved him no matter what he wore, but tonight he looked Montana born and bred.

She watched his hot blue eyes search the room for

her. When he saw her she almost melted from the look in his eyes. He moved toward her, ignoring everyone else. She started for him. But Ryan had seen him.

"I want Zen. Over there." His nephew pointed, drawing everyone's attention. Avery was afraid he'd jump right out of Jarod's arms. It was a good thing he had a strong hold on him. The two men grinned as he handed him over to Zane. "Easy on your uncle, Ryan."

"Hey, sport."

Ryan patted Zane's cheeks and kissed him. It was so sweet, Avery's throat thickened with emotion. "Mama has a baby."

"What's his name?" Zane asked, kissing him back.

"Cole. He wets."

The whole group roared with laughter. Avery followed Zane and Ryan over to Sadie who sat next to Ralph on a chair. He was holding his fussy great-grandson and loving every second of it.

"Do you like your brother?" asked Zane.

"Yes. He cries. He's funny, Zen."

Ralph looked up to see Avery standing by Zane. "There you are, darlin'. Don't you want to hold him?"

"Indeed I do." She leaned over to take the baby. That's when he saw the ring and gazed up at her. "What's this?"

Her pulse sped up. "Zane asked me to marry him. We're hoping for a wedding in three weeks with your approval."

Her grandfather looked overcome, but he got to his feet. At this point Jarod and Sadie relieved them of both children so he could hug the two of them. He wept unashamedly. Avery knew he'd worried about her for years, but no more.

He made a sound in his throat and wiped his eyes. "You and Zane. I've wanted this since you brought our Sadie back home from California."

Zane shook his hand. "I've been in love with Avery for a long time."

"I've wanted it, too, Grandpa. Do you want to announce our news?"

"It would be my greatest pleasure." He moved to the center of the terrace. "Everyone?" he called out, visibly overjoyed. "Tonight is a double celebration. Our family has two new additions. Our little Cole, and Zane Lawson who's going to marry my Avery in three weeks! If only my Myra were here, but I know she's looking on."

The crowd broke into cheers. Everyone mobbed Avery and Zane. But it was Sadie who threw her arms around Avery and cried for happiness. "I love him and I love you. I don't see how life can get any better than this."

"I know what you mean. I love him so much, Sadie."

Cassie was next in line to hug her. "I couldn't be happier for you," she said, her eyes misted with tears. Avery's cousin knew a lot. They promised to get together soon. Cassie wanted to help her with the wedding plans.

It wasn't long before dinner was served. When everyone started eating, Charlo stood up. "Avery is a friend to the Apsaalooké. Tom Medicinehorse is grateful because she found his lost son. Her courage will be remembered. Our people call her Winter Fire Woman."

There was that name again. Avery shivered, wondering what was coming. Zane reached for her hand under the table and squeezed it gently.

"In former times our women related stories around the fire in winter to the families. Then the white man came and asked questions about the stories, but he came in the summer.

"Many of our people believed they shouldn't tell our stories in summer. They didn't want the white man here. Some haven't wanted our stories told at all. They get changed. Avery comes in all seasons to record them and doesn't change them. Winter Fire Woman is always welcome."

His black gaze settled on Avery and Zane. "Yours will be a good union."

Avery got goose bumps. "Thank you, Uncle Charlo," she whispered.

Jarod shot her a glance of pure love and stood up, holding his new son against his shoulder. "A toast to Zane and Avery."

More toasts were offered, and then Zane got to his feet and raised his glass. He had to clear his throat before he said, "A toast to the littlest Bannock who has the sweetest mother on earth. May he grow in goodness and stature like his father, Sits in the Center."

After another hour of celebrating, Zane took Avery aside. "I'd like to stay up all night with you, but an emergency has come up about the case. I'm headed for Billings to meet with Sanders. We're putting a team together to take these people down. I'll phone you when I can."

She squeezed his hand. "I wish you didn't have to go, but I understand. Please be careful."

Zane left her with a hungry kiss before he drove back to his ranch to change clothes and pack up his gear. He'd already swapped trucks with Matt as a precaution to keep a low profile. In a few minutes he had everything loaded, including the bullet that had killed the calf. That was headed for the crime lab stat.

He took off along the fire road. It rose up the mountain and opened up between the trees at one point so you could look down over his pasture. Anyone taking a shot with a rifle would have done it from this spot before driving away in a hurry. He parked alongside the spot and got out with his flashlight and gloves.

A half hour's search didn't yield a cartridge. Here and there he found scraps of paper stuck in the blades of grass. As he was about to climb back in the cab, his eye picked out a wadded piece of foil. He scooped it up and opened it.

A peppermint pattie candy wrapper? He put it to his nose. The mint scent was fresh. Bingo!

Fingerprints or not, this couldn't be a coincidence. Things were falling into place. He bagged it and started the engine. Though he'd told Avery he was going to Billings, he would make a trip to the Pryor reservation first. If he spotted Durant's truck, he could take some dirt samples from his treads and get the results back from the crime lab immediately. The more evidence the better.

But a tour around the settlement revealed no sign of the BIA truck. Durant was out somewhere off the reservation. Four o'clock in the morning everything was quiet. He left and headed to Laurel on the off chance he'd find the missing Toyota on the Newell ranch.

This time he parked just inside the turnoff and crept through a field to stay out of sight. When he was within range of the side of the house, he put on his night-vision goggles and took a good look.

The movement he saw turned out to be the guy who'd been on the tractor the last time he'd come by. His face was a match for Terry Newell. He went into the trailer and came out again with a load of something that he stashed in the Sentra.

After stowing his goggles, Zane took off for the truck. Once behind the wheel he drove down the highway a block, then circled back and parked on the other side to wait. Maybe Newell wasn't coming, but Zane was in no hurry. He drank some coffee from his thermos.

In another ten minutes he saw headlights coming toward the highway from the ranch road. Zane started the engine and followed the car, anxious to trail him to his destination. He phoned local police that he was pursuing a suspect from Old Highway 10 going south on 310 and gave the license plate number. They weren't to close in until the suspect reached his destination.

Another five miles and the Sentra turned off the 310 onto a frontage road. Zane gave the signal. Half a mile farther and the suspect slowed down to stop behind a truck with a janitorial supplies logo. Like a swarm of bees, four patrol cars converged on the Sentra and truck.

The officers told the drivers to step out of their vehicles. Zane climbed down from the truck, flashing his badge. "I'm Special Agent Lawson from the Billings BLM Crime Division office. Are you Terry Newell?"

"*You're* the one who came snooping around our ranch. I haven't done anything wrong."

"You're under arrest for theft and vandalism at three known Crow archaeological sites in the area. Each count carries a prison sentence."

Another deputy had the other driver cuffed. Zane walked over. "You're Steve Newell. I recognize you and your brother from these pictures." He pulled them out of his pocket to show him. "It'll go better for you and Terry if you tell me the name of the mastermind who planned these heists. Blowing up a vision quest fasting site has put you in deep trouble. Maybe we don't have to look any further than your dad."

"He has nothing to do with this."

"You mean he didn't collude with a certain BIA agent who's been helping you boys transport artifacts across state lines? I wonder what we'll find inside this truck. It couldn't be registered to you since you don't work for this janitorial service."

"You can go to hell."

"I'm afraid that's where you're going." Zane nodded to the deputy in charge. "Book him and read him his rights."

Zane walked back over to Terry. "Give me the name of the agents who've been helping you and I'll put in a good word for you with the judge."

"Don't tell him, Terry."

"Do you always do what your older brother says? Can't you think on your own?"

"Butt out, Steve—"

"Shut up, Terry. I'm warning you…"

The guy was vulnerable. "There's nothing Steve can do to you, Terry. But you can help yourself. You're still young. Cooperation will go a long way since this is your first tangle with the law. What do you say?"

He hung his head. "There are a couple of men. Steve only told me one of their names. He said I wouldn't get into trouble if I helped him."

"No, Terry!" his brother screamed at the top of his lungs.

"What is it?" Zane persisted calmly.

"One's called Baxter. I heard him call the other one something like Duran."

"Good. I'll see what I can do for you at your arraignment." He glanced at the deputy. "Book him and read him his rights. I'm on my way to the BLM office in Billings. You can reach me there."

On his way to Billings, Zane got on the phone with Sanders to tell him the latest. They needed another warrant to search Durant's truck and residence for a rifle. If the bullets matched, then he would be charged with more than stealing artifacts. Durant had probably been working with another dirty BIA agent to cover for each other. This was a big crime ring. In time there'd be a lot more arrests.

Sanders couldn't have been more pleased over this major break in a case that had stumped law enforcement for a long time. They discussed the shooting on his ranch and Zane's suspicions that Durant might be responsible for it along with everything else. He reminded his boss of Ranger Margaret Rogers's tip about BIA involvement. He needed to thank her.

"How about that. The lowlife likes peppermint patties. That's a new one," Sanders muttered. He told Zane to mail the bullet into the crime lab, then go home for some well-deserved sleep and they'd catch up later in the day.

Zane drove home to the ranch, happy to obey orders. When he'd gotten enough sleep he'd call Avery and they'd make plans. He couldn't go a day without seeing her.

AVERY TOOK THE day off work and met her cousin Cassie in Billings. They spent all Monday morning shopping for a wedding dress. She'd found a gorgeous white silk and lace princess-style dress that she loved. By saying yes to Zane's proposal, Avery needed to show him she was doing everything to handle her PTSD and be positive. For him, the long white wedding gown would speak more plainly than words that she wanted to be his wife.

Over the past eight years she'd given up every thought of getting married. But when she stood in front of the full-length mirror in her dress with a lace veil over her hair, she felt like a real bride.

It was because of his unconditional love.

Cassie went crazy. "Look at you! Zane will die when he sees you walking down the aisle."

"I don't want him to die, Cassie," she teased.

The shop needed to make a few alterations. Her dress would be ready in a week. Avery felt almost giddy with happiness. They celebrated by eating at a French restaurant. Cassie worried that her brother Ned wasn't making much progress yet. She shared her concerns about her parents' state of mind, and then they drove to the Rafferty ranch.

At two-thirty Avery headed home in her truck, eager to see Zane. He hadn't phoned yet, but she knew he would as soon as he could.

It was only an eight-mile drive back along the winding dirt road threading through the forest before it met with the highway. The day had turned out hot, but it was cooler beneath the trees. When she happened to glance in the rearview mirror, she was surprised to notice a vehicle way back. Where had it come from? That was odd. When she'd left Cassie, there'd been no one else around.

Dr. Rafferty opened up his property for seasonal hunters with permits. His house was set back away from people. The only other road that fed into this one ended up at a closed-off, abandoned logging site. Avery didn't understand it.

She rounded the curves, aware that the vehicle was inching closer. Each time she saw it, she felt a menacing sensation. A dark feeling came over her. Avery knew she was in danger. Her adrenaline started to pump. She rolled up the windows and set the locks.

That old sick uneasiness crept over her and wouldn't leave. It was like the night she'd walked toward her dorm after leaving the library. Though she couldn't see anyone around her, she'd sensed she wasn't alone and she'd started running.

When she'd reached a copse of pines growing at the side of the building, she was grabbed from behind and knocked to the ground. The man dragged her beneath the boughs. Blackness rose up inside her at the memory.

Sweat poured off Avery's body. Terrified at this point, she reached for her phone and pressed five. *Pick up, Zane.* Her heart pounded like a kettledrum. The second he answered she screamed his name.

"Avery? What's happening? Talk to me, darling!"

"Someone's after me, I just know it!" she cried.

"Where are you?"

"I just left Cassie. I'm on the road between the Rafferty ranch and the highway."

"I'm on my way from the house. Stay on the phone with me. I'm calling for backup. Is it a car?"

"No, I think it's a truck, but it's still a ways off."

"Go as fast as you can."

"I am, but they're starting to gain on me. Zane, I'm terrified!"

"You'll be all right. Keep driving and don't stop."

She could barely swallow or breathe. "They're getting closer."

"Can you see who it is?"

"No. The driver's sitting too high in the cab. Oh, no—it's a dump truck! Whoever's driving must have followed us from Billings and was waiting on the logging road until I was alone."

"Stay focused."

"I'm trying, but he's starting to bump into the back of my truck. Zane, he's trying to run me off the road."

"Don't let him do it. Just keep driving as fast as you can. It's a narrow road with little room on the sides. You have the advantage. How close are you to the junction?"

"Maybe three-quarters of the way. He's butting me again—"

"Hang in there. He's doing everything to scare you, but you're still in control. I should be there as you reach the highway."

"Zane!" she screamed. "He just shot out my rear tires."

"Keep going until you can't."

Avery had to grip the wheel with her left hand, but it was impossible to prevent the truck from shimmying around. "I'm going to be sick."

"No, you're not. Grab your gun!"

She lifted her blouse with her right hand and pulled out her weapon, but she was shaking so hard, she could hardly get a good grip.

"Have you got it?"

"Yes, but my truck can't go any farther. I'm stopped. What am I going to do?" she cried. "He's getting out. I can see him in the side mirror. He has a gun. He's the guy who was with Mike Durant at the Rosebud!"

"He doesn't know you're armed. Press your head up against the corner. When he breaks in the window you'll be protected from the glass. Shoot him in the chest or the pelvis."

"I'm petrified."

"You can do it. I'm almost there."

Zane was on his way and he was keeping her sane. Oddly enough Avery wasn't as terrified as the night of her assault. She could see *this* man's face and it was broad daylight. No way was this killer going to get his hands on her. She cocked her pistol.

"Get out of the truck, lady, or I'll have to shoot out the window."

Avery held her breath and stayed pressed up to the corner.

In the next instant, glass shattered. For a second she had a full view of him and shot him, but her body was shaking too hard to get a good aim and she hit him in the thigh. He let out a surprised cry. Then she heard Zane's voice and saw police cars converging.

"Hands on your head, Baxter."

Thank God. Thank God.

He staggered backward, but at the last second he opened fire on Zane, hitting him in the shoulder. While several officers subdued the criminal, Avery screamed and got out of the truck. By the time she reached Zane, they'd put him on the ground. One of the officers was stanching the blood. Another officer called for an AirMed helicopter.

Avery took one look at Zane's colorless face. She cried out in anguish and knelt down next to him. "Please, God. Don't let him die."

His eyes opened and those blue orbs stared into hers. "That's not going to happen. Thank God you're alive and safe. I've just been stunned and I'm going to be fine. Nothing's going to happen to me."

The officer working on him nodded. "He's right. The bullet didn't hit an artery."

"It's a miracle." She grasped his hand and kissed it. "You talked me through my ordeal and saved my life. It's my turn to take care of you. I love you, sweetheart. I won't leave your side."

"Avery…"

Everything became a blur as the helicopter arrived. One of the men found her purse and handed it to her before she climbed in behind Zane's body.

When they landed at the hospital in Billings, he was rushed into surgery. Avery stayed in the lounge and made phone calls to everyone, including her grandfather.

Connor and Liz were the first to arrive. Connor took one look at her and hugged her hard. "Don't worry about Zane. He'll be up and around in a few days. It was only six months ago I had to have an operation on my shoulder. You need any nursing instructions, talk to my wife here."

Liz smiled and gave her a hug. "He'll only be helpless for a few days, then watch out. Most men make terrible patients."

ZANE WAKENED AFTER his operation, but was given a hypo and went back to sleep. When he woke up again, it was the next day. His shoulder and upper arm had been wrapped and put in a sling.

Avery leaned over to help him drink water through a straw. "Good afternoon, my love. Welcome to my world again. You obviously needed the sleep after what you've been through. How do you feel?"

"I'll tell you after you kiss me," he murmured in a husky voice.

She lowered her mouth to give him a brief kiss, but he surprised her with a long, drawn out kiss that took most of the air from her lungs. A flushed Avery lifted her head because a nurse had just come in the room to bring more flowers and check his IV. "I guess I have my answer. Liz told me you'd recover fast," Avery said.

"She ought to know," he teased.

"Your boss came by earlier. He'll talk to you soon but wants you to know you're to take it easy so you'll have a full recovery. Your name is all over the news. According to him, the arrests you've made have led to the capture of Mike Durant and Chris Baxter of the BIA. The ballistics from the bullet proved it came from Baxter's rifle, but Durant was the brainchild.

"Their plan was to kidnap me to bring you out in the open so they could kill you for ruining their elaborate scheme. It's been in progress for several years. They stole the dynamite. On the news they were described as homegrown terrorists.

"What you've uncovered is huge, Zane. You've not only captured the attention of the governor, but the leaders of the Crow and other nations of the High Plains." Her eyes filled with tears. "I'm so proud of you, I can't begin to articulate what I want to say."

She saw banked fire in his eyes. "Don't try. Show me instead."

"I don't dare. That wound needs to heal."

He reached for her hand, fingering the diamond. "I'm planning on the doctor releasing me today so we can go home."

"No, sweetheart. He said the earliest might be tomorrow. It all depends on how well you're healing. He's giving you masses of antibiotics to stem any infection and wants to keep you here just to be safe."

"You'll stay with me again tonight?"

"Where else would I go? We're walking in Liz's and Connor's shoes. Instead of a bull throwing you, a madman shot you."

"I'll take the madman anytime."

She smiled. "To each his own poison."

But he didn't laugh. Instead his features sobered. "You were so brave."

"That's because you had my back through the whole ordeal. I knew you were coming. You helped me keep my head. I've had a lot of time to think about the assault. It forced me to learn to do things to protect myself I would never have done otherwise. By talking me through everything yesterday, you empowered me.

"In some respects I feel like I've thrown off the blackness that has imprisoned me for years." She molded his cheek with her hand. "You've done that for me."

"Then you're not going to back out of our wedding plans because I have a dangerous job to do?"

That was no idle question. He really was worried. His vulnerability caught at her heart. She loved him too much.

"Let me answer you this way. For the past eight

years I've lived with every kind of fear imaginable. But being with you has changed that world for me. To live in fear is death. I've been existing in a walking death state for years. Never again. You make me want to face life head-on. That's what *you* do.

"When you came back from Glasgow, you knew what you wanted and you didn't waste a second. Yesterday you helped me face what I had to do. Your mental strength is awesome. You've shown me the better way to live. It's breathtaking how confident you are. I want to emulate you.

"Yesterday I bought my wedding dress."

His eyes lit up.

"Cassie has helped me make plans. I'm going to be Mrs. Zane Lawson and I'm going to have children with you, provided we're so blessed. I'm not afraid of intimacy with you because I know that with you I'll be safe and cherished.

"But so far all our talk has been about me. At this point I'm concerned about you. I want to take care of you, love. If you'll let me, I want to fill the empty spaces where you've known loss. You've had more than your fair share, but you never complain, never talk about it. Everyone depends on you. The reason they do is because you never let anyone down. You're tough for everyone.

"You have no idea how much Sadie loves you for helping her after her mother died. You were there to give her comfort and love little Ryan when your own heart was broken over your marriage. You helped her through the rough patches with Jarod. You've brought a new happiness to Millie's and Matt's lives.

"My brothers admire you more than you know. You came here and made this land your own. You did it with your own sweat and blood. That's what my grandfather loves about you. You've cleaned out a nest of vipers since you arrived. You've earned your place. If I were Apsaalooké, I'd name you Starts his own Fires."

His eyes had grown moist. "You're well named, Winter Fire Woman. In the winter of my discontent, you warmed me with the fire burning in you. I want to take that fire to my heart and my bed."

"I want that, too," she whispered against his lips. "With time we'll learn to help each other through our episodes. That's what the refiner's fire is all about. Now tell me what I can do for you right now."

"You can lock the door and climb onto the bed with me."

"We'll do that tomorrow after we're home."

His eyes glowed an intense blue. "How are we going to get there? Neither of us has a vehicle here."

"Connor and Liz solved our problem. They pulled his trailer with them."

He reached up with his good arm to draw her head down to him. "I think I feel a heart attack coming on."

"Don't say that. Not even in jest."

"Avery..."

Chapter Eleven

The day before the wedding, Connor and Jarod drove Zane into Billings to get their tuxes and enjoy a last dinner together at the Stockman's Club while he was still a single man. This wasn't your typical bachelor party. Toward the end of the meal, Zane could read the concern in their eyes.

"I know what's on your minds. Believe me, it's been on my mind for weeks, too. And I've been studying up on PTSD—I hope you have, too."

Zane sipped his ice water with his left hand because his right arm and shoulder still needed the sling when he was up and about.

"Avery hasn't actually read the pamphlet I gave you, but I've told her about it." He felt their glances. "Her first response was that it sounded like a blueprint, which, of course, it is. But I believe it's going to work.

"We've had three incidences where she panicked. One in the trailer out at the dig site, and another in the back of the truck the night we were looking for Smiling Face. Both times it was a seemingly innocent touch that set her off. But we were able to recover and talk about it.

"Last night's episode was a little different, though. She'd planned to drive home after we'd watched some TV, but she fell asleep next to me on the bed. I decided to let her stay there and went into the den to get some work done on the computer. Suddenly I heard a blood-curdling scream that frankly frightened the daylights out of me.

"I rushed into the bedroom to find her hunched up against the headboard, sobbing uncontrollably. When I called to her, she looked up at me with a blank stare. For a moment she didn't recognize me. I said her name quietly several times until she finally came out of it.

"I asked her if she wanted to call off the wedding, but she said no and was adamant about it. I phoned Dr. Lindstrom for his advice. Like me, he believes it happened because we're about to take vows, so he's made a suggestion which I've already proposed to her. We're going to have separate bedrooms. For how long no one knows.

"It took tremendous courage for her to agree to our marriage, but the next step is the true test. I've promised her that if all she wants is to be held, then that's what we'll do. Sometimes she's braver about it than other times and has assured me she plans to be my wife in every sense. But after last night I've learned enough about her condition to know there'll be times when she has no control over a flashback any more than I have over my PTSD."

Connor's eyes misted over. "You're incredible, Zane."

"I love her and happen to know you two would do the same thing for your wives under similar circumstances."

"My uncle said her spirit would be freed by one with great vision," Jarod said. "You're like the eagle he spoke of who seeks the deepest blue of the sky. Our sister is the prize and we know she'll be in the best hands with you."

Zane was deeply moved. "I'm a lucky man to be marrying into your family. Thank you for your support."

They returned to the ranch at ten with their tuxes. Jarod drove Zane home. Avery was somewhere inside her house with her grandfather. The two of them had decided they wouldn't see each other until they met at the church. Their wedding was scheduled for eleven the next day. The brunch reception would follow on the terrace of Bannock ranch house. Matt and Millie would be driving Zane.

Once he'd hung up the suit and turned out the lights, he walked out on his patio to breathe in the warm night air. This was his last night having to live alone. Until he'd met Avery, he hadn't given much thought to his aloneness. But now, he hated it. She filled his world. Even if they were going to sleep in separate bedrooms, they were within calling distance of each other and would always be together.

The possibility that she could have been killed by that monster who'd lain in wait for her outside the Rafferty ranch still haunted him. *You've got to let it go, Lawson.*

He went back inside and locked up. On the way to his bedroom he passed the guest bedroom where she would sleep for the time being. He prayed this period wouldn't last a long time. Except for some vases of flowers, he hadn't changed it. That would be up to Avery.

Their so-called honeymoon would consist of them moving in the things she wanted from her house. They would talk about major redecorating, but all in good time. Zane had bought the ranch house as-is after Sadie's father died. Now that he was going to have a wife, they would put their stamp on it.

Deep down Zane was a family man. The joy of knowing their marriage would make a family brought such deep contentment, he moaned for the sheer joy of it. Today he'd purposely avoided coffee so he could fall asleep faster. He hoped it paid off. When he awoke tomorrow, it would be a day like none other.

The house was warm. He took off the sling and went to bed without the benefit of pajamas, something he wouldn't be doing after tonight.

AVERY STOOD AT HER open window, breathing in the air redolent of honeysuckle. It gave her pains of longing clear to the palms of her hands. This was probably the first night since Zane had come home for good that she hadn't been with him for at least part of it. She hated being separated from him.

The gift she'd bought him sat in a little box on the dresser. She walked over and lifted it to the light. A blue topaz as near to the color of Zane's eyes as she could get, was set in a man's gold ring. The artisan on the reservation felt it a great honor to make this for the special agent who'd avenged the enemy of the Crow.

A yearning for Zane stole through her to the point that she couldn't stand it any longer. Forget tradition. She needed to see Zane tonight and give this to him.

Since she was still dressed in jeans and a top, she slipped down the stairs and out of the house to the new truck she'd purchased with Zane. Since she wouldn't be gone long, she didn't tell anyone where she was going.

He'd already given her keys to the house, so if he didn't hear her knock, she could let herself in and call to him. She didn't care if it was close to midnight. Avery knew he wouldn't care, either. It was so awful being apart, tomorrow couldn't come soon enough.

The place was totally dark. Maybe he'd gone to bed. She unlocked the door and walked in. "Zane?" she called to him. "Sweetheart? Are you still awake?"

She heard his voice coming from the other part of the house. Assuming he'd given her the go-ahead, she hurried down the hallway. But she came to a dead stop when she reached the threshold of his room. From the moonlight through the window, his superb body glistened with perspiration. He lay on his back. His sheets were tangled around his hard-muscled legs and he let out little moans that sounded like whimpers.

Zane had told her about his nightmares, but she'd never seen him having one. Her first instinct was to run over and comfort him, but he'd warned her to keep away. Let him wake up on his own time, or talk to him using a soothing voice. The whimpers sounded like he was grieving. It was so gut wrenching, it tore her heart to shreds.

She tiptoed over to his dresser and put down the jewelry box and her keys. Avery must have stood there for ten minutes, but he wasn't coming out of it.

"Zane?" she spoke gently to him. She repeated his name several times. He thrashed around for a moment and then lifted himself up on one elbow. He'd opened his eyes, but he looked disoriented. "Sweetheart? It's Avery. Are you awake yet?"

"Avery?" He sounded incredulous.

"Yes, my love. I couldn't stay away."

"You're alive?"

The question was a revealing one. "I'm very much alive. Let me show you."

"Am I dreaming?"

"No." She moved over to his bed and sat down next to him on his good side. "Lie still." Using the end of the sheet she started to wipe the moisture off his face and chest. Unable to resist, she lowered her mouth to his and kissed him. She went on kissing him until he began to respond. "You see. It's me and I'm here. I brought you a wedding present."

"But we weren't going to see each other until the ceremony."

"I lied. I wanted to come now. Don't move. Let me show you what I brought you." She strode over to the dresser and brought the box back. "It's your turn to open this one."

The lines of stress were disappearing from his handsome face. He opened the box and lifted out the ring.

"I had this made for you on the reservation. My own ball and chain to keep us connected when we're not together. The topaz matches your eyes. Let me put it on you."

She took it from his fingers and slid it home on his ring finger. "You're branded now."

He tried to sit up, but she gently pushed him back down. "I came because I don't want to be apart from you. I don't want separate bedrooms. I want to be with you tonight and every night. Will you make love to me right now?"

"Right now?" His voice shook.

"Right this instant. Contrary to what you believe, I do know what goes on between a husband and wife who are crazy about each other. Tonight you were dreaming that I'd died. I'm here to make that awful dream go away. We have all night to love each other. I'll sneak back to the ranch at dawn. Until then, I need you.

"Forget the blueprint. For my sake you followed it as faithfully as you could to this point. Now we need to throw it away. I love you, Zane. I love you so much."

She took off her sandals and lowered herself to his side.

"What about your pistol?"

"I left it in the truck."

"That has to be the first time you haven't worn it."

"Don't you understand? I've dreamed about being your wife since the first day we met. I've been in agony ever since. Kiss me. Love me. I think I'll die if you don't."

"I want to be your husband first. Tonight let's lie here and hold each other. We'll get to know each other until you're totally comfortable with me. I'm marrying the most honorable woman in the world tomorrow. I want to be worthy of you."

"Oh, Zane—"

He kissed the corners of her mouth. "We're going to enjoy ourselves tonight. I promise. But we'll save the best until we're officially together. Now come here to me, Avery, and make my dreams come true. You're the only one who can."

She launched herself into the arms of Starts his own Fires.

That's what he did, and no woman on the planet would ever know the degree of her joy.

* * * * *

Watch for Cassie and Trace's story
in the final installment of Rebecca Winters's
HITTING ROCKS COWBOYS miniseries,
coming April 2015
only from Harlequin American Romance!

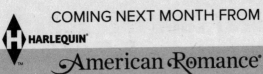

REQUEST YOUR FREE BOOKS!
2 FREE NOVELS PLUS 2 FREE GIFTS!

 HARLEQUIN®

 American ★ Romance®

LOVE, HOME & HAPPINESS

YES! Please send me 2 FREE Harlequin® American Romance® novels and my 2 FREE gifts (gifts are worth about $10). After receiving them, if I don't wish to receive any more books, I can return the shipping statement marked "cancel." If I don't cancel, I will receive 4 brand-new novels every month and be billed just $4.74 per book in the U.S. or $5.24 per book in Canada. That's a savings of at least 14% off the cover price! It's quite a bargain! Shipping and handling is just 50¢ per book in the U.S. and 75¢ per book in Canada.* I understand that accepting the 2 free books and gifts places me under no obligation to buy anything. I can always return a shipment and cancel at any time. Even if I never buy another book, the two free books and gifts are mine to keep forever.

154/354 HDN F4YN

Name	(PLEASE PRINT)	

Address		Apt. #

City	State/Prov.	Zip/Postal Code

Signature (if under 18, a parent or guardian must sign)

Mail to the Harlequin® Reader Service:
IN U.S.A.: P.O. Box 1867, Buffalo, NY 14240-1867
IN CANADA: P.O. Box 609, Fort Erie, Ontario L2A 5X3

Want to try two free books from another line?
Call 1-800-873-8635 or visit www.ReaderService.com.

* Terms and prices subject to change without notice. Prices do not include applicable taxes. Sales tax applicable in N.Y. Canadian residents will be charged applicable taxes. Offer not valid in Quebec. This offer is limited to one order per household. Not valid for current subscribers to Harlequin American Romance books. All orders subject to credit approval. Credit or debit balances in a customer's account(s) may be offset by any other outstanding balance owed by or to the customer. Please allow 4 to 6 weeks for delivery. Offer available while quantities last.

Your Privacy—The Harlequin® Reader Service is committed to protecting your privacy. Our Privacy Policy is available online at www.ReaderService.com or upon request from the Harlequin Reader Service.

We make a portion of our mailing list available to reputable third parties that offer products we believe may interest you. If you prefer that we not exchange your name with third parties, or if you wish to clarify or modify your communication preferences, please visit us at www.ReaderService.com/consumerschoice or write to us at Harlequin Reader Service Preference Service, P.O. Box 9062, Buffalo, NY 14269. Include your complete name and address.

HAR13R

"Kiss me." He leaned close to the window to give her prime access.

"Why would I want to do that?" Suz's blue eyes widened.

"Because I have nice lips. Or so I've been told. Pucker up, dollface."

"I don't pucker for anyone who calls me 'dollface,' unless you want me to look like I bit into a grapefruit. Now *that* kind of pucker may be available to you."

He laughed. "So much sass, so little honesty."

She sniffed. "I'm trying to *save* you, cowboy, not romance you. Don't confuse this."

He sighed. "No kiss? I really feel like I need to know if you're the woman of my dreams, if you're determined to win me. And a kiss tells all."

"Oh, wow." Suz looked incredulous. "You really let that line out of your mouth?"

"Slid out easily. Come on, cupcake." He closed some distance between her face and his in case she changed her mind. *Strike while the branding iron was hot* was a very worthwhile strategy. It was in fact his favorite strategy.

"If I kiss you, I probably won't like it. And then what motivation do I have to win the race? I'd just toss you back into the pond for Daisy."

He drew back, startled. "That wouldn't be good."

Suz nodded. "It could be horrible. You could be a wet kisser. Eww."

"I really don't think I am." His ego took a small dent.

"You could be a licky-kisser."

"Pretty sure I'm just right, like Goldilock's bed," he said, his ego somewhere down around his boots and flailing like a leaf on the ground in the breeze.

"I don't know," Suz said thoughtfully. "Friends don't let friends kiss friends."

"I'm not that good of a friend."

"You really want a kiss, don't you?"

He perked up at these heartening words that seemed to portend a softening in her stance. "I sure do."

"Hope you get someone to kiss you one day, then. See you around, Cisco. And don't forget, one week until the swim!"

Don't miss
THE TWINS' RODEO RIDER
by USA TODAY *bestselling author Tina Leonard!*

Available February 2015,
wherever Harlequin® American Romance® books
and ebooks are sold.

www.Harlequin.com

Love the Harlequin book you just read?

Your opinion matters.

Review this book on your favorite book site, review site, blog or your own social media properties and share your opinion with other readers!

Be sure to connect with us at:
Harlequin.com/Newsletters
Facebook.com/HarlequinBooks
Twitter.com/HarlequinBooks

HREVIEWS